UNHINGED

THE EBB AND FLOW OF MY UNRULY LIFE

SANJAY KUMAR PANDEY

Contents

Contents

Part I

I

My First School

I had set the mosquito net on fire. I was furious. Why wouldn't Ma take me to the hostel despite having promised about a week ago that she would take me there next week? I was just six years old and believed 'hotel' and 'hostel' were the same places where I could dip my hands into shiny, large glass jars and take out namkeens and sweets to relish them without any restrictions.

Ma came rushing. She was frightened. She immediately took me into her lap and speedily moved away from the burning net to the far end of the corner of the room. Soon, my Mama, a 25+ young, bespectacled man who was younger than Ma by more than 10 years, burst into the room excited. On finding the net burning and the fire spreading like wildfire, he immediately rushed outside and was back in a moment with a bucket of water that he had fetched from the nearby hand pump.

Then, before wasting any time, he excitedly began to throw jugs of water on the fire, which, by now, had spread further, and was threatening to turn the entire room into dust and ash. Soon, he managed to douse the fire, but not before it had already done its job--turned the entire room dirty black.

He was furious when he learnt what I had done. Looking at me with his large, bespectacled eyes burning with anger, he screamed, "Are you mad?"

"Shohan, calm down; he is just a child." Ma tried to pacify my agitated Mama, who was seething in anger and highly agitated about what I had done. Without saying anything further, he left the room in a hurry in an extremely excited state, but not before he had cast yet another angry 'how could you be so stupid and set your own house to fire' look at me.

When the situation had normalised after some time, the room cleaned, and the charred mosquito net thrown into the already overstuffed pink dustbin placed outside the room, near the main entrance, taking me into her arms, Ma asked me calmly, "How the fire broke out, beta?"

A little frightened and badly confused about what I had done, I explained everything. She listened to me with marked interest. But, surprisingly, she didn't scold me. Looking at me for a moment with an unexplained smile, Ma just wiped my face with her orange-colour cotton saree, hugged me tight, and kissed my forehead.

The next day-on a clear wintry morning, when the air was dry and cold, around 8 AM I found myself at the Bagaha bus stand. At that early hour, there were only about half a dozen people at the almost deserted bus stand. After waiting for about 40 minutes, she boarded a Bihar state transport bus to Bettiah with me. During those days, Ma--a primary government school teacher--was posted in Bagaha--a sleepy town located in the West Champaran District of Bihar.

Bagaha is well-known for its stunning natural beauty and historical importance. Placed at a distance of 35 kilometres from Valmiki Nagar, where Ma Sita is believed to have lived with her two sons—Luv and Kush--after being expelled from Ayodhya by Lord

Rama, Bagaha is strategically located at the meeting point of Bihar, Uttar Pradesh, and Nepal. Champaran occupies an important place in India's history of the freedom movement. It was from there that Mahatma Gandhi began his freedom movement to liberate the country from British rule.

"Where are we going, Ma?" Looking outside the half-open window of the speeding bus, I cried enthusiastically. I was elated as I had a window seat and I could see the stunning views outside easily while the soothing and fresh, cold wind beat against my face and hair sending a surge of happiness through my excited body.

"We are going to Betiah. You want to study in a boarding school, and live in a hostel, right?" Ma responded, looking at me with a mysterious smile. Though I didn't then know what boarding school meant, I was happy that my dream of living in a 'hostel' and enjoying the goodies was going to be realised soon. I was on Cloud Nine; I looked at Ma with happiness and gratitude.

It took us around two-and-a-half hours to reach Betiah—the administrative headquarters of the West Champaran District in Bihar, located near the Indo-Nepal border, roughly 225 kilometres away from Patna, the state capital. During those days, it had many good schools with boarding facilities for young students.

By the time we reached St. Hilarion Academy--the place where I was to spend the next year of my early life--I was already asleep, I had no idea in whose lap. I have no idea how she carried me. I was awakened by a male's voice and was surprised to find a tall, somewhat handsome man with grey hair and large eyes looking at me with deep curiosity.

I was deeply startled, almost scared. There was something disturbingly outrageous about that handsome face. I glanced at Ma with a questioning look while keeping a wary eye on the person from the corner of my vision.

"He is the principal of the school where you would study. Now he will take care of you." On getting no response, she continued, "Be a good boy and study well; I will visit you next month."

Then, after completing the admission formalities, and depositing the school and hostel fees for the year, she left me with a heavy heart. I detected she had tears in her eyes. For the first time, she had put me in a boarding school.

But I was happy when she left. I looked around with curiosity and excitement. A whole new world awaited me--a world where I could eat whatever I wanted. All I had to do was dip my hands into glass jars and take out whatever I wanted. But where were those shiny, big jars about which I had fantasized a lot? Before long, I realised that I had been put in a 'hostel' for study purposes, and there was a BIG difference between a 'hostel' and a 'hotel.'

I have a hazy memory of the time that I spent at my first school though I do remember that our days at the boarding school started with a prayer followed by breakfast with rotis/bread, aloo ki bhujia, boiled eggs, and milk porridge. Then, we were handed over to different teachers who taught us different subjects in the brightly painted classrooms.

Ours was a reputed Christian missionary school in the area. So, a visit to a neighbourhood church every Sunday was a regular affair for every student, including non-Christians, like me. There, we were taught about the beauty of Christianity and how it has the power to shape the world--for the better. We were told that only Christianity has the power to show humanity the right path. So, everyone should surrender to Christ and walk in his footsteps.

At that age, I didn't understand what religion meant. However, it felt good to visit the beautiful stone & brick church in sparklingly clean, nice clothes every Sunday; and see a large number of neatly turned-out men and women attending the Mass, making interesting cross signs, and reverently kissing the cross dangling from their necks. The brightly painted church with a HUGE cross at its top was visible from far away.

Other than the regular visits to the church every Sunday, what I remember about my stay at the boarding school was the monthly visits by my maternal uncle, who was younger than my mother by a couple of years. At that time, he was around 27-28 years old and unmarried. He was tall and a little dusky. He was a clerk in the State Bank of India (SBI) and was posted at Bettiah.

Whenever he visited me, I remember he took me out for a couple of hours and treated me to some delicious goodies, including heavenly butter buns and delicious jalebis. No wonder I always looked forward to his visits, though he wasn't regular with them and visited me only when Ma coaxed him. Perhaps, he didn't like being my local guardian as it tied him somewhat and restricted his bachelor movements.

Ma often chided him when he failed to turn up at my school and felt he wasn't properly doing his duties – that of being my local guardian and taking care of me. On the occasions, when he did not visit me, I became depressed and spent my time sulking alone in my dormitory, watching squirrels and birds playing hide & seek on the nearby trees whose swaying branches caressed the window panes of my second floor dormitory.

When after a couple of months, Ma realised that he wasn't interested in visiting me, a little irritated, she spoke to my Mausa, my mother's younger sister's husband, and asked him to visit me, at least every month. "Visit him at least once every month on Parents' Day so that he doesn't feel alone and becomes depressed; he is just a child."

My Mausa was a fairly good-looking young man in his late 20s. During those days, he was employed as a manager at a local inn in Motihari--my maternal father's hometown. I still remember that the inn had a large stuffed tiger displayed in its lobby. It looked intimidating; the first time I saw it, I ran to Ma and hid behind her, scared.

My Mausa, the youngest of five brothers, was from Bhagalpur and worked in Mothari. He had married my youngest aunt--a tall, thin woman in her early 20s, just a year ago. Being younger than my Ma by several years, he respectfully called Ma 'Didi.' So, when Ma asked him to become my local guardian, he couldn't refuse. He started visiting me every month on 'Parents Day'. I regained my happiness and began savouring my favourite butter buns when he took me out for a delicious treat.

II
My Early Years In Patna

Soon, my stay at the school came to an end as my father had taken voluntary retirement from the army and started living in Patna at his ancestral house. He wanted the family to stay together.

My father was a very fair and rather tall man. Nicknamed 'Bhura Pehelwan,' he was a wrestler in the Indian army and looked frighteningly strong with big paws and pillar-like thighs. He always kept a khukuri (a kind of small sword with a distinctive recurve in its blade) hidden under his bed and exercised vigorously every day, early in the morning.

I often heard interesting and eye-popping stories about him and learned how, on certain occasions in the past, he had put the fear of God in some people by charging at them menacingly, flashing his khukuri in his gigantic right hand, when they had come charging late into the nights to forcefully occupy our ancestral house after the premature death of my grandfather.

My grandfather was an affluent Mahant; he owned many

properties, pieces of land, and a sprawling two-floor house, neatly divided into two sections, in the city near the Patna Railway Station, where he lived. For his vast property and wealth, he was poisoned by my step-grandmother-a dusky woman with humble origins. After the premature death of my grandmother--who was extremely fair and from a well-off family-- before I was born, my grandfather came into contact with the woman who later became my step-grandmother, and she started living with him.

When my father learnt about his father's sudden death, he was posted somewhere in Kashmir, near the Indo-Pak borders. He took a long leave from the Army and left for his house in a hurry. When he reached Patna, he learnt what had transpired in his absence. Hot-blooded that he was, he immediately drove the intruders out forcefully and regained his ancestral property. My step-grandmother had illegally sold off the house to a local muscleman for a small amount after poisoning my unsuspecting grandfather and leaving the house with someone earlier with her three kids.

In Patna, I was enrolled at a reputed day boarding school called St. John's Academy, along with my elder brother, who was four years older than me, and my younger sister, who was younger than me by one year. Here, I studied for close to four years. During this period, we often bunked our classes and spent our school time visiting the Patna Zoo and the Ganges Ghats.

One reason for visiting the zoo was that it was HUGE, with plenty of greenery and fruit-laden trees. We often brought all sorts of fruits that we could lay our hands on from there and gave these to Ma, who believed that we had bought them with the pocket money that she gave us daily. The reason behind visiting the Ghats was that it offered us an immense opportunity to savour the sweet jalebis and delicious pooris from the nearby roadside eateries.

For a long time, our parents had no idea where we were spending our time during school hours. Our secret was out when, one day, my father caught us red-handed loafing around the river ghats when he went there with someone known to him to buy green bamboo for the upcoming Hanuman Jayanti. Like most wrestlers, he was an ardent devotee of Lord Hanuman and bought a new green bamboo every year to hoist Hanuman Pataka on the occasion.

That day, we got a severe beating that kept our young limbs sore with pain for several days. As our crime was BIG, Ma didn't interfere, and so we had no escape from our father, who, for long, thrashed us with his large–sized palms. My parents were furious with us because they thought that some untoward incident might have occurred and we may even have drowned in the deep Ganges waters as we time and again bathed in its waters with gay abandon without any elders around.

From that day onwards, we didn't bunk any classes and went to our school regularly. To ensure that we weren't back to our old, errant ways and we weren't bunking our classes, Ma visited our school principal almost every fortnight to make enquiries about us.

III

Life in the Sainik School

I was quite a good student and did well in school. No wonder my parents had high hopes for me. After the exams were over, my Ma, being rather forward-looking and ambitious, put me in Sainik School Tilaiya (SST), in Hazaribagh, after I successfully cracked the entrance examination in 1983 for the prestigious school that admitted only 60-odd students out of 1000-odd aspirants every year.

I still remember vividly that my parents were on top of the world when they found my name on the list of successful candidates. My overjoyed father fed pooris and bhaaji to the beggars at the Patna Hanuman Mandir, located near the Patna Railway Station.

The year 1983 is special in my life for a different reason also. During the same year, while I cracked the tough entrance exam of the celebrated school, our cricketers--led by the indomitable Kapil Dev at Lord's, England--defeated West Indies in the finals of the Prudential World Cup to lift the Cup. It was no small feat at that time. For the first time in the history of the apex international tournament, India had won the much-coveted cup. The icing on the cake was that it had beaten the mighty West Indies Team that had several globally renowned and much feared cricketers, like Gordon Greenidge, Michael Holding, Desmond Haynes, Viv Richards, Andy Roberts, and Malcom Marshall.

No wonder the air, across the country, was thick with happiness and pride, and the different key heroes of the tournament-Kapil Dev, Mohinder Amarnath, Sunil Gavaskar, Sandeep Patil, Syed Kirmani, Kris Srikkanth, and Roger Binny—became household names overnight.

My tutor, who had tutored me for the SST exam, was equally happy. "India is changing and is poised for growth. You are also changing. SST will change your destiny," he exclaimed, beaming with happiness and pride the next day when he came to our house to give us tuition. I then didn't understand how winning the Cricket World Cup would change the fortunes of the country. I didn't understand this or how SST would shape my destiny for the better and propel my career. I don't know if the win in the World Cup helped India in a big way, but my admission into SST indeed was a landmark development in my life; it changed me and my life in several ways, perhaps for the better.

I was in SST for five years, from the sixth to the 10th standard. Those were the most constructive and life-changing years of my life. The rigorous routine and life at the school, located at the foothills of the picturesque Kodarma Dam, completely changed my life, and with one stroke, I became the apple of the eye of my family, neighbours, and relatives.

"You are a special and gifted kid; you have made the entire locality proud by making it to the finest school in Bihar on the basis of your talent and hard work," they frequently told me. We also had many visitors from my locality and nearby areas, and they congratulated my beaming parents and told them that they had raised brilliant kids. My parents naturally felt proud of me and showered love on me when I visited them during the summer and winter vacations. My elder brother, though, didn't seem pleased with the special treatment given to me, and he grumbled when my parents pampered me. It was difficult for me to understand why he behaved in such a way, but that's how he was.

It was perhaps because he considered me his gotiya- a rival and competitor for our parents' resources and love. He believed that with him around, I had no right to be pampered and showered with so much love and affection. He often snapped at Ma, asking why she visited me on Parents' Day and why I didn't stay in the boarding school even during the holidays, though Ma rebuked him for this, crying, "Don't forget that he is your own blood, your own younger brother; don't say such nasty stuff about him."

At school, I was good at boxing and debates, and I represented my house successfully many times. In studies, though, I wasn't good in most of the subjects, except English and Biology—the 2 subjects in which I, in fact, mostly did well even without studying much. I loved English because I felt it needed to be mastered to excel in life. I loved Biology because it gave me a chance to study human and plant life and their many wonders. My natural passion for these subjects and the ensuing high performances in them, coupled with my innate excellence in boxing and debates, endeared me to most of my seniors and teachers, who considered me an asset and a special talent.

When I started winning inter-house competitions in these two easily, year after year, while my father, teachers and seniors rejoiced, my Ma didn't seem to be too happy as I wasn't doing well in most of the other subjects. "Focus on studies; boxing and debates won't take you far in my life," she often told me. At such times, though, my father came to my rescue and disarmed her, asserting, "Let him do well in whatever comes naturally to him. Besides, it's good that he is doing so well in boxing. He is a strong and healthy boy." Since he himself had been a very successful wrestler while he was in the army, he was elated; his son was walking in his footsteps and hammering his rivals effortlessly, like him.

Thanks to my excellent boxing and debate skills, I became quite popular in my school and was often praised by my seniors and house teachers as I helped my house, i.e., Mithila, gain important points and trophies several times. During those days, my school had 10 Houses, including Mithila, Pataliputra, Vaishali, Magadh, and Kunwar Singh.

Throughout my stay for five years in the school, I didn't lose a single bout in the boxing ring. So feared and flawless, my boxing skills had come to be recognised that I was even pushed to represent my house across higher weight categories in boxing. As boxing came naturally to me, I kept my successful journey in the ring and continued to win laurels for Mithila and my team. On certain occasions, when my opponents learnt in advance that they would be fighting against me, they panicked and requested me not to thrash them in the ring and just mechanically win and leave them without swollen & bleeding faces and/or broken & mutilated noses.

Being friendly by nature, more or less of the same age as them, I, I mostly did as asked, though on one occasion when I didn't fight, befitting my skills and background, one such person wrongly believed that he could take on me successfully and possibly even come out victorious. The incident took place in July. It was a pretty hot day, and the Sun was shining a little above the heads of those who had turned up to watch, dazzling their eyes with its bright, searing rays.

For the said match, as promised, initially, I just went through the motions without thinking and didn't hit him even once, the way I normally did, but egged on by his friends and seniors, he kept on scoring valuable points against me. During those days, boxing bouts in our school had three rounds of two minutes each, and points were awarded on the basis of the clean hits made at the different permissible areas on the body.

At the end of the first round, while my teammates and seniors were attending me and wiping my face clean with a wet towel, looking at me a little perplexed, they cried with a frown, "What the hell are you doing? What has happened to you? Why aren't you fighting the way you normally do? With such a shabby performance, you will lose the match!" This set an alarm in my mind.

Before leaving, they added, angrily looking at my opponent being attended in a similar way at the other corner of the ring, "This idiot is scoring valuable points, and he is way ahead of you. He is just a fly before you. Squash him!"

This made me furious. I looked at the boy, who seemed to be pretty comfortable and happy with his performance so far. When our eyes met, he stole a quick glance at me that seemed to make fun of me. I understood at once that he was a cunning fellow who had played with my emotions and tricked me, and if I didn't fight the way I normally did, I would end up losing the bout and the match.

"He won't last for the final, third round; I will knock him out right away." I had made up my mind. So, when the bell rang for the second round, I charged at him right away and savagely like a wild and over-excited bull, and even before he could understand what I was up to-I hit him in his face from the left with a savage uppercut.

So powerfully and with so much strength, I had hit him that for a moment, he shook like a leaf in a storm. Then, suddenly, he dropped to the floor like a log and lay sprawling on it as if his life had been drained out of his unresponsive body. He couldn't stand on his feet before the ageing, pot-bellied referee counted 10, and so I was declared a winner with a knock-out performance before the crowd of my beaming housemates, supporters, and others.

After that eventful incident, for several days, whenever he came across me or crossed my path anywhere in the school, in the playground or in the classroom, he made all efforts to avoid me and looked the other way when he noticed me looking at him. Deep inside, he knew well that he was the culprit - and not me. Still, for some unexplained and mysterious reason, he continued to hold a grudge against me, and till the time I was in the school, he never spoke to me.

I made no effort to break the ice either. "Why should I reach out to him when he doesn't wish to do so?" I thought with hostility and anguish though I would have preferred had we started talking again as he was a nice boy and I loved having him around. Sometimes, one unpleasant small incident severs healthy relationships forever, and no matter how many years pass, the situation remains the same.

Other than this incident, I also have a vivid recollection related to one of my close friends, Mihir Thakur. He was from my house, Mithila and was my best friend during those days. He was from Madhubani—located about 170 kilometres from Patna, which is famous across the world for its ancient art, known as Madhubani Painting.

He loved devouring the sweet and syrupy dry fruits and Khoya-stuffed gujhias that Ma sent for me when she called on the 'Parents' Day every month. I loved him for his friendly and affable nature. He was a studious and disciplined boy, and I was a carefree person who was more into boxing and debates. We were nicknamed Heer-Ranjhaa by our fellow students as we were inseparable, but it didn't bother us, and we continued to be often seen together, much to their annoyance.

Once, maybe out of jealousy, some such boys at the school tried to create a wedge and sow the seed of misunderstanding between us. They got a chance to do what they wanted when, once, as usual, I was selected to represent my house in the inter-house debate competition. Mihir was keen to participate and represent Mithila, but since I had a better voice and had been representing our house in debates and declamations successfully over the years, Mihir was ignored, and I was picked up by my seniors and teachers to represent our house, as usual.

Sensing an opportunity, the boys poisoned Mihir's ears, saying, 'He has played politics to scuttle your chances. You consider him your friend, but see what he has done? Is he really your friend?' Mihir sulked for many days and even began to avoid me. But we soon became thick once again, and the designs of the boys to separate us fell flat. Until I was at Sainik School, he remained my best friend. I lost track after a couple of years, though, after he successfully cracked the UPSC exams and started working for the Ministry of External Affairs of the Government of India. The last time that I heard about him was when he was posted somewhere in Chile, South America.

Part II

IV

The Delhi Chapter

I was at Sainik School Tilaiya for five years. I left it after completing my 10th exam, as I was keen to go to Delhi for further studies. I had heard a lot about Delhi from some of my seniors who had visited it: how 'happening' it was and how it had no dearth of pretty and incredibly voluptuous Punjabi girls. Such tales often fuelled the wildest imaginations of the boys, including me, and I decided to move to the capital, like many others, after my board exam.

So, soon after the exams were over, I expressed my desire to my parents and told them that I was keen to continue my further studies in Delhi. Initially, they were hesitant, but they relented when I convinced them that I would study hard, prepare for the prestigious Civil Services Exam, and return as an IAS officer from there.

I also told them Delhi had excellent coaching centres and career opportunities for bright students. Being simple and trusting people, they didn't make further enquiries little realising if a person was unable to do well in the best school of Bihar that had ample of facilities for such endeavours how would he do the unthinkable from a new place, all alone.

Ma requested one of my distant maternal uncles to take me to Delhi and enrol me in a good public school. My uncle, who was always neatly turned out, was employed with the railways. Using the Railway Travel Pass, he took me to Delhi on the scheduled day.

I was euphoric. It was my first visit to the capital, about which I had heard and read a lot. When we got down at the New Delhi Railway Station, after an 18-hour long and tiring journey, I was very tired. For the first time in my life, I had travelled so far. The station was a sea of humanity, and the huge, surging crowd overwhelmed me.

Later in the day, after we had a quick breakfast of pooris and chole, he took me to Colonel Satsangi Kiran Memorial (CSKM) School, located in Satbari, near Mehrauli, close to Rajeev Gandhi Farm House. It was run by an ex-principal of Sainik School Tilaiya, Colonel Satsangi, and I had its address. The sprawling school was tucked away neatly in a semi-rural area in a corner of South Delhi. We reached the place after we boarded a rickety Delhi Transport Corporation (DTC) bus from Mehrauli.

I was there for 2 years and completed my intermediate from there. The school offered me an opportunity to explore Delhi and its many wonders quietly and secretly. I repeatedly bunked my classes and crept out of the school silently. I went to New Delhi, Connaught Place, and Chandini Chowk areas to watch movies of all kinds and enjoy Punjabi food, for which Delhi is known across the country.

Ma sent me money regularly every month, and I used a sizeable chunk of it for certain purposes she wouldn't have approved of had she learnt about them. I didn't miss a single movie that was shown in these areas across various theatres, such as Golcha, Regal, Odeon, and Shiela. I was in love with Delhi and its life, which gave me a chance to enjoy movies and delicious roadside food, not stop. Chole Bhature, Bread Pakora, Chai, Dal Fry, king-sized Samosas topped with dark brown choles and fragrant green & red chutneys,

Tandoori Rotis, Lemon Soda... I savoured it all and returned to my school stealthily in the late evenings.

For a long time, the school management didn't notice my absences, but soon, it was found, and I was taken to task. The school principal called me to his sprawling office. "Where have you been going quietly without informing us?" the retired army colonel, with a soldierly face, grey moustaches, and whiskers, was angry. But I was ready with my answer. "I have been visiting my local guardian who lives in Paharganj," I returned with a blank face, looking straight at him. "But you should have informed us in advance." This is all that he said that day, and he lost interest in the matter thereafter. The school management didn't seem concerned, or it felt the need to seek further details.

Emboldened from then onwards, I started leaving my school openly whenever I wanted and returned a happy and satisfied person late in the evenings. Till the time I was there, my parents had no idea what I was doing in Delhi with their hard-earned money.

V

The First Great Prize of My Life

After doing my +2 from the CSKM Public School, I left it to pursue my further studies at Delhi University. On the suggestion of a person named Jay Prakash Gupta, who was from Patna and doing his Ph.D at the South Delhi-based Jawahar Lal Nehru University (JNU) during those days, I rented a room in one of the official flats on the university campus for Rs 300. It was a princely amount during those days.

The spacious white and brown painted first-floor government building located opposite a small park had two rooms, plus one drawing room and was occupied by a Malayalee family from Kerala. I was given one of the inside rooms whose window opened towards the park. It gave me a good view of the greenery and the playing kids. The government property had a common bathroom and an Indian toilet adjacent to the drawing room.

Since I was just a young boy and remained mostly outside throughout the day, they had no problems sharing the house with me. The owner's wife, a stocky woman in her late 30s, gave me a large puffy idli and a steaming cup of coffee daily in the morning, which I loved to savour. They were a pretty nice family and seemed to be fond of me. One reason could be that I was incredibly fair and good-looking during those days and looked quite innocent as well. Till the time I was there, I enjoyed my stay there, under the umbrella of their affection and kindness.

Other than the steaming cups of coffee and puffy and soft idlis that I still remember relishing while I was their tenant, there was another thing that has been etched on my mind. Once, there was a visitor who had come all the way from Kerala to meet my landlord and his family. She was a relative of my landlady from her home state, Kerala. She stayed with them for about a month. The woman was of medium height and was married. From the day she landed, I noticed she was interested in me and lost no opportunity to talk with me and touch me at the slightest of pretexts. On such occasions, my young, still-growing body burned with an unknown desire, and I felt good to have her around me.

Her name was Meghana. She was a little womanly thing in her late 20s. Like typical South Indian women, she was dusky and amply endowed and had generous hips that swayed with a rhythm when she walked. She had a nice figure; even though she wasn't tantalizingly voluptuous, she was pleasingly plump and good-looking. She had large eyes that she always kept kohl-lined. She always had a smile on her face and often threw casual glances of interest at me and looked happy to have me around.

I secretly envied her husband- a young, dark-complexioned, hollow-cheeked, moustached man in his early 30s who joined her after a few days. After his arrival, she became a little reserved, kept a distance from me, and always seemed to be occupied with her husband and her sister-in-law (my landlady).

One day, I noticed her packing her bags with her husband and learnt later that she would leave for Kerala the next day. A spasm of pain shot through me. I was a miserable person; I became heartbroken and sulked the whole day. I didn't even relish the idli and coffee that day brought by my landlady and hoped against hope that Meghna wouldn't leave and that her trip back home would get cancelled.

Women have a sixth sense; they know what's occupying a man's thoughts. Perhaps she had read my mind and knew I liked her but wasn't happy with the new development. The next day, while I was asleep, there was a soft knock on my door. It was a cool winter morning, and the clock had not struck 7:30, when I usually left my bed. Rubbing my eyes and flinging a shawl around me hurriedly, I opened the door with a yawn, half asleep. Meghna was standing outside with a steaming cup of coffee and a soft, jumbo-sized idli. She offered me those with a searching look.

I took what she had brought and was about to shut the door mechanically when putting her right foot forward, preventing the door from shutting, she brought her face close to me and whispered in broken Hindi, "What's wrong with you? Are you unwell?" A little taken aback by her unexpected, bold behaviour, I remained quiet for a moment. Then, suddenly surcharged with pent-up emotions, I winced like a wounded animal, and even though I made vain efforts not to shed tears, I couldn't help showing one or two.

It had a startling effect on her; she immediately entered my room and closed it softly. I was taken aback. "What would her husband and others think?" I wondered with unease. But she looked unperturbed and completely at ease. As if she had read my mind, she said, "Don't worry; nobody is in the house; they have gone out for a walk." Her eyes glittered as she spoke. Then she added hurriedly, a little alarmed, "But they will be back soon." She looked at me, waiting for my reaction. On finding none, she said softly, "I like you, and I know well that you, too, like me." I remained quiet.

She continued, "We will leave for Kerala today in the evening, and perhaps I won't be able to see you again."

I was still quiet and was now looking at the opposite grey wall with Buddha painting vacantly. By now she had come closer and I could smell the intoxicating fragrance of her skin and the jasmine oil that she had generously applied on her hair. I could also see her deep cleavage girdled by generous, soothing mounds that lay half exposed now as her saree had slipped a little giving me a peek of her soft breasts. My eyes grew bigger.

She had noticed where my roving eyes were resting. Smilingly, she took me into her embrace and planted a kiss on my unsuspecting, virginal lips. Her breath burned on my face, and I got crushed under her inviting breasts and soft, burning cheek. As if spellbound by her womanly charms, I unknowingly buried my face in the middle of her breasts and inhaled deeply. These were soft and inviting like the idlis that she had brought for me. We remained locked in a tight embrace for almost five glorious minutes.

Then, suddenly, she broke free when she heard the sound of the fast approaching footsteps. And, before I could say anything, she quickly tidied her saree and left me, but not before she had cried softly, "I love you; you will always be special for me." Then she was gone.

Meghna left that day for Kerala in the evening, leaving me buried in my insurmountable grief. After about a week, I left my accommodation and rented a new place; I had become miserable in her absence in my old accommodation, as it strongly reminded me of her and made me sad. She was the first great prize of my life.

VI

My First Heartbreak

After moving out of my first rented accommodation in Delhi, I rented another place nearby and also enrolled for further studies at Delhi University. For some strange reasons, I opted for Distance Education mode to do my graduation. Simultaneously, I also began looking for part-time job opportunities to earn some extra money and spend my time productively. Though Ma sent me enough money every month, I reasoned there was no harm if I earned some extra money to support my new life and growing expenses in the metropolis.

I soon found an opportunity in the Sunday Edition of the Times of India. There was a short advertisement that read, "Wanted young boys and girls to work for 14 days for a South Extension-based garments shop. The selected people will be paid Rs 100 per day. Tea and Lunch will be provided free." I was intrigued. I went to the place the next day and got the job right away. I was elated. It was a princely amount. One could live off the amount with comfort for 2-3 days in Delhi. During those days, while a cup of tea cost just Rs 1, a plate of chole bhature cost just 3.

When I arrived for work on the chosen day, I was surprised to find a fair and cute girl of medium height sitting near the cash counter of the shop. She had an uncanny resemblance to the famed Bollywood actress Mumtaz. She had the same short nose and naughty face and was well-endowed at all the right places, like the famous Bollywood actress who made a handsome pair with the matinee idol Rajesh Khanna in the 70s and delivered many memorable hits with him, including 'Roti,' 'Bandhan,' and 'Saccha Jhutha.'

I learnt later that her name was Seema, that she had joined as a summer salesperson, and that it was her first day at the shop. Ours was a group of 5 girls and 2 boys. Apart from me, there was one boy of my age. And, talking of the girls, apart from Seema, there were 4 girls. They all looked pretty, but no one came close to Seema in terms of attraction and womanly appeal.

Seema knew that I was interested in her; in fact, everyone at the shop knew this and they frequently teased me for this. While at such times I felt a little uncomfortable, Seema looked completely unperturbed. She actually appeared to be least bothered. I took it as a sign of her interest in me. I didn't know at that time that she wasn't interested in me at all and was just having fun at my cost.

Throughout the fortnight that I was employed there, everything was in a stir at the shop; there was constant coming and going, and everyone seemed to be very busy. How the two weeks came to an end in a whiff, I don't recollect precisely, but soon it was time to say goodbye. While others who had joined us, like me, seemed to be happy, I was miserable. After getting paid, everyone, except me, left one by one.

I stayed over for about an hour more in the shop chatting with the owner, a talkative middle-aged Punjabi woman, and I left after getting paid by her. Later, after a couple of days, I tried contacting Seema several times, and I even went to her house to express my love. However, I wasn't prepared for what greeted me. She was furious; she gave me a piece of her mind before her confused parents. "Why have you come here? We don't work anymore together, right?"

I was hurt and didn't know what to say or how to react. Her parents tried to cheer me up as perhaps they didn't want a scene at their house. They had understood that we were together earlier but after the job got over Seema had decided to move on. Her father afterwards dropped me at the society gate and gently but firmly asked me not to bother them again.

He was dark-complexioned navy personnel of medium height and seemed to take a lot of pride in his official white navy uniform. My sudden arrival at his place hadn't gone down well with him. So, he was pissed off. Had I lingered on for some more time at his place, he would have possibly lost his temper, and the situation might have gotten out of control.

As I had no desire to witness such a scene, I left the place with a heavy heart. For the second time in my young life, I had heartbreak. "Seema has walked out of my life, or was she never a part of my life in the first place?" I wondered later, a little confused. However, I soon forgot her as life awaited me in all its glory and I had no time to cry or lose my sleep over spilled milk. I was just 22; my whole life lay in front of me, waiting for me with open arms.

VII
My Mother

My mother was a religious person. She kept fast for two days every week and often went on extended religious tours to distant parts of the country with some of our neighbours and family members from her mother's side. By the time I was 25, she had visited most, if not every, religious destination. From Vaishno Devi to Kedarnath to Tirupati to Jagannath Puri-not a single such place escaped her religious fervour. And the ones that she hadn't managed to visit yet were high on her wish list of must-visit places.

One such place was Mount Kailash and Manasarovar Lake in Tibet. She was keen to visit it and often asked me to find out the route and the tour process. Being located in a sensitive zone near the Indo-China borders, at a very high altitude, one had to first get a medical certificate from AIIMS, Delhi, to get valid permission to visit.

During those days, a mythological TV series on Lord Shiva was also being shown on TV. My parents watched the show daily without a break and followed what was shown. When, in one of the episodes, Ma Parvati discussed getting her son Ganesha married, as he had reached the age for marriage, my mother watched aptly.

Later that day, I overheard her telling my father, 'We should get him married as he is now over 25. Let's perform our parental duties; even Ma Paravati says that parents shouldn't keep their children of marriageable age unmarried for long and get them married without any delay.'

The next day, I heard her speak to some of her relatives and office colleagues that she had a son of marriageable age who studied in Delhi and prepared for Civil Services. After a week or so, one of our neighbours contacted Ma and spoke about one such match.

"They are from Chapra. The girl's mother is a government employee and works under the Block Development Officer (BDO) at Baniyapur in Chapra. Her eldest daughter would be a fine match for your son."

My visibly happy Ma asked her to ask the girl's parents to visit them.

The next day, we had two visitors—a woman around 44 and a gentleman in his early 50s. We came to know later that the woman was the mother of the would-be bride and the man was her distant maternal uncle. When my parents introduced me to them, they took a liking to me at once and gave me 2100 rupees as their blessing. I wasn't too keen to accept the money, but they insisted, saying, "It's our ashirwad, beta." They stayed for an hour, during which they had several cups of steaming chai and hot samosas with my parents, which my elder brother had brought for them from a nearby sweet shop.

When they finally left, Ma came to me beaming. She was excited. "What is the matter, Ma?" I asked curiously. She said nothing but patted my head and left me humming a popular film tune from an old Rajendra Kumar movie. She had a habit of humming popular Bollywood songs when she was happy.

"Have they fixed my marriage with the girl whom I haven't even seen?" I wondered, a little worried. But I didn't press the matter and left for Delhi after two days (I was on holiday to spend my time with my family in Patna).

After roughly a fortnight, I received a registered post from my mother. It looked quite heavy. I was curious. When I opened it, two postcard-sized pictures of a young girl with little pink lips popped out, catching me by surprise. Inside, there was also a letter in Ma's neat handwriting. It said they had fixed up my marriage with the daughter of the woman who had visited us when I was in Patna a couple of days back, and the two photos inside were of the girl whom I was supposed to marry.

I was stunned; I stared at the photos absent-mindedly for a few minutes. The girl looked homely. She had big dove-shaped eyes and was nicely endowed. Still, I don't know why I didn't like the fact that my parents had fixed my marriage without even bothering to seek my consent. Besides, the girl didn't fit the image of the girl I had in my mind as my future wife.

Ma's letter further said that I should visit Patna within a week as the girl's family wanted to perform the sagai (engagement) ceremony. Now, this was too much. Not only had my parents fixed my marriage, but they had also decided to move so fast. For the first time in my life, I was angry with Ma. I didn't call her for almost a week. Earlier, I regularly called her almost every second or third day late in the evenings as long-distance calls during those days were little cheaper after 8 PM.

Ma called me after a week, but I didn't answer her call even though my visibly irritated landlady, a tall and full-bosomed jat woman in her early 40s-on whose landline number my mother had called-repeatedly asked me to receive her calls. "What's wrong with you? Why aren't you responding to your mother's calls?" She said angrily when I was going out for dinner that day. I didn't say anything and quietly shut the main door gently from outside, leaving the woman scowling behind.

I received a registered post from Patna after three days. It was addressed by my Didi. She insisted that I visit Patna without further delays, and respect my family's wishes. I was under a lot of pressure. While I didn't want to get married soon - that too with a girl who wasn't my type – it was difficult for me to ignore my family's repeated calls and letters.

When the pressure became unbearable, and I could take it no more, I booked a train ticket to Patna and left hurriedly for my home town by Vikramshila Express after 3 days. I wanted a way out by having an honest and open conversation with my family. I didn't wish to hurt their sentiments. However, at the same time, I didn't want them to sabotage my life and career either. I was determined to stay single for at least the next 4-5 years.

Throughout my 14-hour-long journey, I kept wondering why my family members were in such a hurry to get me married. I also wondered why the girl's parents were eager to marry their daughter off when she was hardly 16 or 17 years old. When I dozed off on my upper berth in the train, lost in such thoughts, I had no idea, but when I awoke early in the morning the next day, the fast-speeding train had already left UP behind and entered deep into Bihar and reached Arrah.

Situated just 55 kilometres away from Patna, Arrah is located on the confluence of the Ganges and the Sone Rivers. The Lion of Bihar, Veer Kunawar Singh, the renowned freedom fighter who gave the British Empire a tough time during the first war of Indian independence in 1857, was from Arrah. I hurriedly put on my shoes and washed my face before having a steaming cup of coffee brought by the smiling, bald train vendor.

VIII

The Last Months of My Bachelor Life

I, indeed, had an animated conversation later in the evening after reaching my home town, completely exhausted by the long and tiring journey around 1 PM. This is an altogether different matter that while my parents and family were happy to see me, they weren't in any mood to heed my repeated and persistent entreaties as they had already made up their minds.

My father, in fact, looked irritated. "If he doesn't get married to this girl, we won't make efforts again for him in the future." He cried, throwing up his hands in the air. He had a scowl on his face, and I fancied a glimpse of hatred for his favourite son on his face.

When I hesitatingly requested him to think again about the matter and not get me married hurriedly, he dismissed me with an impatient wave of his hand. "We have made up our minds." He said with a resolute tone. I knew that everything had been suddenly and irrevocably decided. So, after tossing up in my bed uncomfortably for a long time that day, I gave up in dismay and decided to go ahead with my family's plans. However, I was determined to meet the girl at least once before giving my consent.

With this thought in mind, like a man condemned to death, I went to my parents' room in the evening. Finding them sharing their thoughts on some important subject, clearing my throat, I said, "Okay, since you all have already made up your mind, without thinking of your son's well-being and happiness, at least allow him to meet the girl!" Taking a dignified pause, I added, "Whom he is supposed to marry against his wishes-at least once."

Though my father looked hesitant and non-committal initially, nudged by my mother, he agreed after looking at me for a few minutes with an indescribable expression. Later that day, my mother spoke to the girl's mother on the phone in the evening and conveyed the message to her. After two days, I found myself with my family at a hotel located near the Patna Railway Station where the girl's mother had brought my future wife.

Beaming with happiness and pride, the girl's mother---whose aged face still retained traces of her former beauty--showered us with several gifts, including an expensive gold ring, branded suits for me, high-quality silk sarees for my mother and my sister-in-law, and imported shirts and trousers for my father and my elder brother. They also presented my family with several boxes of sweets and dry fruits.

While my family was totally won over by their hospitality and was visibly moved with happiness, I wasn't, and this clearly reflected on my disappointed face. The bride's mother was a little worried. "What happened," she asked my Ma later. Ma tried to divert the attention by saying, "Nothing, he is a little tired after such a long train journey from Delhi." We left after an hour but not before my would-be mother-in-law had extracted a promise from Ma that we would agree to an early marriage. Perhaps she had sensed something was amiss and thought that it was better if there were no delays from our side.

I learnt later from my wife that my mother-in-law had already made up her mind to get her daughter married to me, no matter what. According to her, it was a very good match and 'Made in Heaven.' In her over-enthusiasm and eagerness to get her elder daughter married to a boy studying in Delhi, who she believed would one day be either a SP or a DM, little did she know then that marriages solemnised in a hurry and without the full consent of the two parties-especially the boy and the girl-often crumble like a pack of cards.

After a week, I returned to Delhi upset. I was a completely changed person by now. I knew my days of freedom were about to end soon; so, I wasn't happy. The enthusiasm for life had somewhat vanished and I had become less ambitious.

As planned, the date of my marriage was fixed by the girl's family after consulting with my family, and I was asked to return back to Patna after just 20 days for the BIG DAY. When I reached Patna by Magadh Express, after a delay of nearly nine hours, I was exhausted in every limp. It was already 9:30 PM, and the vendors and shopkeepers in my area were shutting down their establishments or clearing away and packing up their wares.

But on reaching my home, I saw, with profound amazement, my entire house wearing a festive look and brimming over with my family and relatives. Right from my beaming sisters with their husbands & kids in tow to maternal uncles with their families to distant cousins, almost everyone had turned up in style for the marriage.

Strangely, while everyone looked happy and excited, one of my maternal uncles didn't seem happy with the match. The next day, while I was having tea on my balcony, I overheard him telling my mother, "Didi, cancel this wedding on one ground or the other; it's still not very late." He looked a little worried.

'What happened? What's wrong with them?' Though Ma looked worried, I also noticed that she had a frown on her face. She was a little annoyed with what her younger brother had said.

"I don't know, but cancel the programme; it's still not too late." My bespectacled uncle with henna-dyed hair repeated with a grave voice, and then soon afterwards, much strangely, he broke into hysterical laughter. My eyes sparkled in the exuberance of my new found joy. Finally, there was a ray of hope for me and there was at least one person who shared my thoughts. I thanked my uncle in my heart with gratitude without saying anything.

However, though initially, Ma seemed to be a bit disturbed, she soon brushed aside her worries and decided to go ahead with the proceedings, much to my dismay and to the utter disappointment of my uncle. Had she listened to her brother's advice that day, intently and trustfully, the whole thing wouldn't have horribly gone so wrong later.

On second thought, who knows what the future has in store? What Ma couldn't see at that time, my Mama had, perhaps, already seen as he had a deep knowledge of astrology; he could predict with a great deal of accuracy what lay in the future.

Part III

IX

The Marriage

The marriage rituals continued all through the night, ending with the usual seven pheras in the early morning. Throughout the proceedings, my bride remained huddled quietly beside me while two of my maternal sisters watched us with an all-knowing smile. By the time the rituals ended in the wee hours of the morning, the next day, I was almost starved. As per the custom, both I and my bride had to fast till the pheras (it's an important ritual in an Indian wedding, the ritual of walking around the holy fire, agni, or another sacred object or idol) had ended.

Soon afterwards, my mother-in-law escorted me to the room, where I found a plate full of pooris, sabzi (vegetable curry), sweets, and dahi-vadas waiting for me. Though I was famished, and the food looked quite tempting, surprisingly, I couldn't bring myself to eat what lay before me. Sensing that I wasn't keen to eat, she insisted, "Eat at least a little beta; Maya will eat the rest."

In India, especially in rural areas, it's customary for the wives to eat the food left by their husbands. Besides, a bride can eat ONLY after her groom has eaten. Had I not eaten, Maya, too, would have gone hungry. So, for the sake of the poor girl, I ate a poori and some parwal-aloo curry that was heavily spiced. Then, after washing my hands and mouth and touching the feet of my mother-in-law, I left in a hurry to join my family, neighbours, and relatives who had been accommodated in two sprawling govt. School buildings nearby.

We left Baniyapur, Chapra, after a few hours with the bride. I was a changed person. Now, I wasn't alone; my wife was with me. I don't know why, but I felt a little weighed down and utterly tired from the new development in my life. We reached Patna late in the evening, incredibly exhausted. After the usual rituals related to the welcoming of the bride had been performed and food eaten, while my tired guests and family members retired to their respective rooms and beds, I was told to go to my wife, who was waiting for me quietly on the bed prepared hastily for us by my mischievously smiling sister-in-law.

My sister-in-law--a small woman with a pair of sunken eyes, who limped a little while she walked, thanks to the presence of a steel rod in her right thigh--pushed me into the room, saying, "Maya seems to be an unopened bud; have fun." Then, she walked away, giggling like a schoolgirl towards my maternal sisters, whose attention, I spied, was riveted upon me. This greatly embarrassed and disconcerted me. Evading their prying eyes, I shut the door quickly. Then, turning my back toward the closed door, I walked unsteadily and nervously towards my saree-clad waiting bride, who was sitting in the corner of the bed in the dimly lit room with her face partially covered by the pallu of her maroon and red coloured saree.

This was the important moment about which I had heard and seen (in the movies) so much. I was fed on this faulty idea that "billi ko pehli raat ko maarna zaroori hota hai." (It's important to sexually dominate your bride on the first night to set the template for the rest of your life.) So, after talking with her a little about the weather and the tiring journey, I soon tried to get down to the job that was expected--hurriedly, without much ado.

Though I didn't have a good idea as to how to go about the whole thing, as it was my first encounter of such a kind with a woman, I did have some inkling about the whole thing. So, dipping into whatever little and half-baked knowledge that I had on the subject, I started the 'thing' with trembling hands, shaky confidence, and blurred vision. She turned crimson and surrendered her inexperienced body to my equally inexperienced hands. Since both of us were complete novices and had almost no knowledge about the whole thing, it turned out to be disastrous, and I ended up making a mess of the BIG NIGHT.

To add to my woes, Maya, by now, had sensed that I was a complete novice like her and was fumbling badly. Much strangely, this aroused her motherly feelings for me; she relaxed, and her stiff body opened a little. I have always noticed that women have a tender heart; their maternal feelings set off when they sense someone needs their help and kindness.

She became confiding and warm and a smile began to flicker on her soft face that glowed in the dim light of the pink-coloured room. Then, after looking at me with the entire love of the world in her dove-shaped eyes, she lurched forward, and took me in her warm and fleshy arms, before she suddenly planted a wet kiss on my unsuspecting, almost virginal face.

It had an electrifying effect on me, and I instantly had a lump in my throat. My emotions welled up suddenly and a feeling of deep possession seized me with a frenzied energy. "She is mine, only mine," I murmured fervently. With this, I also regained my confidence and my hesitation went away instantly. I returned the favour with passionate kisses all over her face. She giggled and snuggled close to me. We felt good to envelop each other in a tight embrace.

When and at what time we fell asleep together--I have little or no idea. We were woken up the next morning by a loud noise. Someone was impatiently and violently tugging at the handle of the door of our room. Rising hurriedly from my bed, I looked at the wall clock. It was already 9 a.m. When I opened the door sheepishly, rubbing my eyes, I found one of my maternal uncles (the youngest of the three brothers of Ma) and Ma standing at the door, looking worried.

They were soon joined by my sister-in-law and maternal sisters, but they didn't look worried, and they had an all-knowing, mischievous smile. Before I could say anything, while Ma and my uncle left quietly, my sister-in-law and maternal sisters barged into the room uninvited and sat on the bed near my wife. "How was the night? Did bhaiyya trouble you?" Maya didn't respond, though she snuggled close to my sister-in-law with a smile.

After two days, my parents threw a grand reception for the guests and relatives, besides the neighbours. In our area, the reception organised to welcome the bride is called Bahu-Bhaat. A large number of our relatives, friends, and neighbours turned up for the occasion. Maya's mother and maternal aunt had also arrived, and they had brought expensive gifts for me and my family.

My wife's mother had worn a red salwar-kameej and appeared as if she had landed at our place for the occasion-straight from a beauty parlour. She had decked her up, especially for the occasion, and I noticed, much to my discomfort, some of my relatives throwing curious glances at her. When Ma complimented her for her beauty, dress sense, and make-up, my wife's bua (aunt) suddenly murmured loudly somewhere from behind, "boodhi ghodi, laal lagaam."

My wife's bua--a somewhat tall and dusky woman, who was a government employee, lived in Gopalganj (a tiny hamlet located in the Goplaganj district of Bihar) with her husband and three children. She had a sneer on her face and looked a little irritated with my mother-in-law for arriving decked loudly for an occasion that demanded her to dress up appropriately, befitting her age.

Still, we were somewhat taken aback by this public display of ridicule for Maya's mother. However, and very surprisingly, her jibes had little or no effect on my wife's mother, who, unmindful of her jeering, continued to pose confidently for the pictures with everyone. We later learnt, over a period of time, that she had developed a thick skin and never took jibes targeted at her to her heart. She sported cropped hair and wore jeans. She went on long tours with her male colleagues to the distant parts of the area, unmindful of what others said about her.

We also learned later, through some common sources, that she frequently spent several days alone with some of her chosen bosses, including the BDO and the Block Doctor of the place where she was posted and where she had been assigned government accommodation. I found it somewhat strange that while publicly she almost ignored her husband--a tall and half-bald man about 50 years old, who reminded me of a famous Bhojpuri actor--she went out of her way to please these two people and others who were her seniors. In fact, she seemed to worship them and bend backwards to miss no opportunities to please them and keep them in good humour.

X

The Secrets of My Mother-in-law

My mother-in-law was a junior officer (adhikari) and was posted with the Chapra sub-division. Her duties saw her travel to Chapra City and other areas nearby on and off. She always looked much in command and happy with the area's BDO, a tall, gray-haired person, and the Block Doctor, a white-haired, somewhat thin gentleman. She regularly left our house late in the evenings to spend time with the doctor and returned only the next day in the early morning hours.

Her secret outings seemed to trouble my father-in-law not because he didn't like his wife spending her nights with her seniors but because he feared that I would find out the 'secret' one day if she didn't rein in her frequent late-hour adventures. I, indeed, learned the 'secret' one day; this changed my--and their lives-- forever. It also signalled the end of our beautiful and strong relationship.

It all began with me asking my wife pointedly one day, when we were alone and taking a walk near our house, "Where does your mother go during the nights and return the next day in the mornings?" She was taken aback by this unexpected question thrown at her out of the blue and didn't answer me for a while. When I repeated my question, this time a little pissed off, she responded with a quavering voice, "She goes out for important official work." I noticed she was avoiding my piercing eyes. She looked uncomfortable.

"C'mon, tell me the truth. Do you think I am a fool," I was very irritated by now. This terrified her and she responded with the truth after sometime during which seemed to be battling with her thoughts. "Ma is in a relationship with the BDO and the Block doctor." I was stunned. My worst fears that my mother-in-law wasn't a normal woman and a devoted wife had come true.

Walking slowly and without any purpose, my wife continued, "This has been going on for long"...she paused for a moment and then, with much difficulty, added, "What can we do?" By now, she had turned round and burst into a flood of self-sympathetic tears. The brutality of her sorrow continued to distress her for almost an hour. Afterwards, it wore itself out, and she became a little calmer and more collected. I remained quiet throughout the period as I had no desire to stifle my love for her and witness a fresh surge of grief from the blameless and pure girl.

Deep inside, I knew that she was a good girl born but born and brought up by morally corrupt parents. I use the word 'parents' because I soon learnt that her father, too, was equally sinner as he was in an open relationship with the maid of the house. He, in fact, was a bigger culprit as he indulged in moral debauchery with the maid right inside his house.

The maid's name was Reena, a stout girl around 24 years old. She was the daughter of the local dhobi--a sickly, rat-faced, dark-eyed person--and was employed as a maid to do the regular household work, like scrubbing and cleaning, for them. She, over and over again, stayed with my wife's family and ran the household affairs the way she liked. She, in fact, behaved as if she owned the house. My wife and her younger sisters lived in constant fear, and they seldom did anything that ran the risk of irritating her. I found the whole thing somewhat strange and wondered why no one--especially Maya's father--said anything to the person who was just a petty servant.

But I soon got my answer. Reena was my father-in-law's pet and mistress. He was a morally corrupt person like my mother-in-law with the only difference being that while my mother-in-law fulfilled the desires of the BDO and the Block doctor outside of the house, my wife's father did the same, right inside their home with Reena as her partner though he was careful not to attract 'unwanted' attention from others, especially from me.

But this 'family secret' was out one day. I was at my in -law's place with my wife in one of the rooms located at the far end of the three-room official quarter allocated to my mother-in-law. It was a scorching June afternoon, and everyone was inside their rooms, sheltered from the harsh and unforgiving heat. Hot and unforgiving wind still managed to enter the house from some of the exposed and open areas and troubled the people inside. My father-in-law was in the drawing room and seemed to be reading a newspaper, and Reena was busy in the kitchen doing something. My wife's two younger sisters were sleeping uncomfortably in the adjacent room.

After some time, I felt the need to use the bathroom located at the other end of the house. To reach it, one had to pass by the drawing room. As I was about to pass by the room, I suddenly heard someone giggling. I immediately turned my head towards the place where the sound was coming from. It was coming from the drawing room. When I peeped inside out of curiosity, I was shocked to find the maid sitting on my father-in-law's lap and laughing while he held her in a tight embrace. They were in a 'different' zone, unmindful of their surroundings.

I hastily pulled back to my room, unnoticed. For a long time afterwards, I remained in a state of violent agitation and didn't even drink the sherbet (cool, flavoured drink) brought by my wife after some time. When I could take it no longer, I erupted before her after my father-in-law had left for the weekly market and the maid had gone to her house in the evening.

"What's going on in your house?" I was furious. "What...I don't know what you are talking about?" Maya responded a little confused. "So, you don't know?" I interrupted her with disgust and anger. By now, she had, perhaps, figured out that I had seen what I wasn't supposed to see in her house. So, she remained quiet with a strained look on her visibly terrified face.

"Your family is rotten; had we known the kind of family that you have, we would never have agreed to this marriage." I was seething with anger. This was indeed too much for me. Both my mother-in-law and my father-in-law were openly having extra-marital relationships despite having grown daughters and their son-in-law around. My wife stole a glance at me. On finding me in a highly agitated state, she continued to remain mute. That night, I tossed uncomfortably in my bed with anger and unbearable summer heat for a long time.

I left Baniyapur the very next day early in the morning in haste for Patna though I was supposed to stay for at least a week at my in-law's place. I didn't even meet Maya's father and mother, who, at that time, were outside, and were arriving hurriedly to see me off to the bus stand.

While on my way to Patna, I was in great turmoil and seethed with anger. I kept thinking about what I had done to deserve such a rotten and morally corrupt family. By the time I reached Patna, I had become ill with thinking. I was livid with my family for having hastily married me off without checking the family background of Maya's family, and so I decided to give them a piece of my mind. I reached Patna late in the evening, dead-tired. Almost every body part throbbed with pain. The rickety bus had journeyed through pot-holed and badly kept Bihar roads to take the travellers to their respective destinations.

Later, while I was having my dinner, Ma asked me, "Is everything okay, beta?" She looked worried. She had sensed that something was seriously wrong. I didn't say anything and kept eating quietly; I didn't wish to say anything before my sister-in-law and brother, who were around at that time, as they would have used it against me in the future to mock me for having such relatives. As Maya's family had given several expensive items and gifts as dowry for this marriage, my elder brother and sister-in-law weren't happy. My brother especially felt let down for not being fortunate enough, like me, and not getting married into a relatively well-off family.

However, when they had gone away and I found Ma alone, I erupted, "You have ruined my life." After waiting for a while, I narrated everything to her with such bitterness and anger that Ma was shocked and pained beyond any measure. Surprisingly, she didn't say anything to me or ask any questions at that time, and she left me quietly.

The next day, however, after we had breakfast of triangular paranthas, bhujia, and dal, and the dining table had been cleared, and everyone, except Ma and me, had left, she said to me, "Beta, I am responsible for this mess. I should have checked their background." Then, after a brief pause and looking at me with a questioning look, she asked, "How is Maya? Is she like her parents?" "Of course not! Why and how would she be like them?" Much to the amusement of Ma and my surprise, I was furious with Ma for asking such a disturbing and insulting question about my wife.

"So, it means that she is completely different and not like them; it also means that you love your wife," Ma was smiling by now. She looked pleased with both the information and the realisation that her son loved his wife. By now I had become a little puzzled though.

"Beta, ignore what you have learnt and seen at your in-law's house and focus ONLY on your wife." On getting no response, she added, "She is pure, like Tulsi." Then, taking a deep breath, she added, "Catch the first bus to Chapra tomorrow and bring her here before it's too late." On finding me listening to her with wide eyes and full attention, she continued, "After a few days, take her to Delhi with you."

As Ma was a religious and good woman, she didn't want the poor girl to suffer due to her parent's moral debauchery. She possibly believed that if we removed Maya from her corrupt family, everything would become fine once again, and we would be able to save the marriage, which was on the verge of collapse, thanks to the discovery of the uncomfortable truths.

How wrong this God-fearing and unsuspecting woman was!

XI
Trouble in Paradise

I went to Baniyapur the very next day. Maya was overjoyed to see my return so soon. My in-laws didn't seem to share her enthusiasm when they learned about the purpose of my unexpected visit. By now, they had perhaps figured out that I had learned about them. However, they behaved as if everything were normal, like before.

The very next day, I boarded a bus from the Chapra Bus Stand and returned to Patna late in the evening with my elated wife. All through the seven-hour long journey by bus, she held my hand in her hand and looked into my eyes with her dove-shaped eyes. She was in love with me madly, but so was I.

When we reached Patna, it had become somewhat dark, and we were awfully tired. My mischievously smiling sister-in-law opened the door and welcomed us with a grin. Maya immediately touched her feet and sought her blessings. Then we went inside and found my Ma and father watching TV. Ma broke into a big smile and showered her blessings on us.

Then--after we had taken a shower to wash-off the dirt and the grime that had stuck to us like a leech, thanks to the long and tiring journey over muddy and broken roads--we had our dinner. I noticed that Ma was beaming with happiness and had prepared a special sumptuous meal for us with ghee-smeared rotis, dal tadka, baigan bharta, rice, salad, papad, and kheer.

We stayed in Patna for a week, during which Ma took us through several religious rituals for the homecoming of the bride. We left for Delhi by Rajdhani Express on the date decided earlier. My parents had booked tickets on the luxury train for us as it was my first trip by train with my wife, and they wanted to make us as comfortable as possible.

In Delhi, for the next couple of months, everything seemed fine, and we enjoyed our honeymoon period, lost in each other's arms. We were madly in love with each other and had almost forgotten our bitter past. However, this marriage 'wasn't made in heaven;' it was 'destined to crumble.'

It all started with my wife getting a call from her mother one day. It was sometime during the month of September. The weather was pleasant, and there was a bite in the air. While the summer season was on its way out, the winter season was about to creep in stealthily and slowly.

Maya informed me later that her mother and younger sister were planning to visit them next week. Though I wasn't happy with the unexpected and unpleasant news, for the sake of my wife, I didn't say anything that may have punctured her happiness. She seemed to be happy and looked forward to meeting her mother and sister after so many days.

They arrived the next week, as planned, and stayed with us for 3-4 days, during which they visited some places in the city with my wife and returned late in the evenings. I had no idea that with my mother-in-law and sister-in-law, the BDO, my mother-in-law's boss and lover, had also landed in Delhi, though he was staying in a city hotel somewhere near the New Delhi Railway Station.

I had no idea for many days that my wife had accompanied her mother and sister to the hotel on two successive occasions. I learnt about this only later, after my mother-in-law and sister-in-law had left for Bihar. But when I learned about this accidentally one day, I got choked with rage at myself. The news pained me so much that I felt as if a nail had been driven into my skull. I also felt outright useless.

"Why the hell your mother's boyfriend was here?" I exploded, confronting my wife in the kitchen, where I found her preparing food for the evening. At that time, she had her back towards me. She immediately turned startled, almost terrified. I noticed that her face was white, and her upper lip was twitching. Her lovely face had terror written all over it. When she noticed that my eyes were red with rage and my teeth clenched with hatred, she became very nervous.

Taking a step back as if to protect her from my sudden and unexpected outbursts she began to cry. However, her tears had no effect on me; in fact, they added fuel to the fire of my anger. Lurching forward towards her menacingly, I shouted, "Why did your mother take you to him to the hotel where he was staying?" As she had no words to explain, she kept on looking at me in fear and sobbing non-stop. This somewhat brought the level of my anger down, and I said calmly, "Tell me everything honestly, and I will forgive you!"

This relaxed her a bit, but she didn't respond right away, as if she were weighing her thoughts and wondering if she should disclose what had transpired. Then, after wiping her tears with her dupatta and breathing painfully, she said, "Ma wanted me to make him happy." She had a searching look on her face now. I felt numb; a searing pain shot through my whole body, paralysing me from my head to my toes. After a pregnant pause, she added, "But I refused flatly!" Then, looking at me with pleading but searching eyes, she cried, "Trust me, I haven't hidden anything from you!"

"How was the experience of pleasing a man old enough to be your father?" I observed harshly with my lips twisted in a scornful smile. I found myself roused to a maddening fury by now. "What? You don't believe me?" For a moment, she looked at me with anguish. Afterwards, she suddenly clutched me and gazed despairingly into my eyes. When I shrugged her off with disgust and anger, she started crying again. She was soon drowned in her tears and was violently shaking with sobs.

I patiently waited till her sobbing had died away. Then, with much bitterness, I snapped at her, "C'mon, do you think I am a kid; you will go to meet your mom's lover secretly and spend time with him in a hotel, and I will think that you have gone just for a courtesy visit? Am I a fool? No, I am not, though I was a fool earlier, and I believed in you and your innocence. How stupid I was?"

She burst out crying again. Her cries and my loud voice had been heard by our neighbours by now, and I heard someone quietly open a door nearby. This embarrassed me, and I immediately put a break on my outburst and left the house quietly, evading the prying eyes of my immediate neighbour--an intrusive, stout Marwari woman in her early 40s--who, who I found was standing at her door looking at my house intently and trying to hear every word coming out of it.

I returned late in the evening from my office that day and didn't eat anything, despite Maya asking me for it many times. I noticed that she also hadn't eaten; she wailed through the night, though in a low voice. I couldn't sleep either and kept on tossing in my bed uncomfortably till late into the night. I sank into a deep, sound, and refreshing sleep when it was already morning.

I woke up late, and I immediately glanced at the wall clock; it was already 10:30 AM, and the Sun was shining brightly into the room at that hour, throwing a bright ray of light on the left wall and the corner near the window. After having a cup of ginger tea with rusks with my wife, I asked Maya to call her father. When she cried with alarm about what the matter was, I didn't say anything. After some time, I asked her again clearly, calmly, and resolutely to do what I had asked her to do. She sighed as if she was lost in her thoughts and grief and gave me no response.

Since she was unwilling to call her father, I spoke to him directly later that day, "Please visit us within the next 3-4 days and take Maya with you." When he asked what the matter was, I interrupted rudely, "Please just do it!" I then disconnected the phone, ignoring my wife's request not to ask him to visit Delhi in such a manner so abruptly.

He came after two days. "What happened, beta? Is everything okay?" My tall father-in-law had a questioning look on his face, and he seemed a little worried. I didn't say anything about what had transpired. I observed, "Actually, I have to go to Bangalore for a week for some official work." I screwed up my eyes and paused for a moment, and then added, "Since it would be difficult for Maya to manage on her own, it would be better if she would be with you while I am away." Afterwards, evading the eyes of my highly disturbed wife, who was looking at me with a pained expression, I continued, "I will bring her back after I return from Bangalore!"

My father-in-law looked at me for some time, startled and wondering. Though he wasn't satisfied with the explanation, he didn't say anything further. He stayed at my house for three days before he left with Maya. During this period, Maya kept on pleading, when her father wasn't around, with folded eyes and tears in her eyes, not to send her away to her home like this. However, I remained entirely unmoved; I had made up my mind. I was convinced that she wasn't anymore pure for me, and I needed to cut her from my life for the sake of my sanity and well-being.

Strangely, she didn't say anything to her father about the whole thing while they were in Delhi. Maybe she was worried about the effects. Though he himself was a man with loose moral values, had he learned that Maya's mother had brought her boyfriend to Delhi, and taken Maya to his place twice secretly, he would have lost his cool, and the whole thing would have spiralled out of control.

They left on the fixed date by Vaishali Express from New Delhi Railway Station. With it, I heaved a sigh of relief. When I bade them goodbye at the overcrowded railway station, I knew well that it was the last time that I was seeing them, and this wrung my heart. I loved my wife, but for her own sake and my mental peace, it was better if we ended the relationship.

Maya kept on looking at me from the moving train window with a beseeching look till I had become a tiny dot on the platform, and she had lost my sight, and I could no longer hear the deafening noise of the fast-speeding train engine. I felt lifeless, like the platform now. Till the time the train was at the platform, the whole area throbbed with noise, energy—and life. With its exit, the entire energy and life seemed to have been sucked away from the area. In a similar way, till my wife was with me, I felt full of life and energy.

I received a call from her the next day. But I didn't respond. She called again later in the evening; I didn't respond, like before. She called again the next day and several times over for the next couple of days. But I continued to ignore her, like before. I had steeled my mind and had thrown out of her life. I was dead sure that she wasn't pure anymore; she had been sucked out of her purity and innocence by my mother-in-law's partner and by perhaps several more people like him.

I write 'several more people' because I received a call from my mother soon after Maya had left me. Ma informed me that she had a visitor, a woman in her early 50s from Maya's village, who advised her to end the relationship for the sake of her son, i.e., me. She informed my mother that some people, known to my mother-in-law, often visited their house late in the evenings when Maya was around, and they left the next day early in the morning. Most such people were high-profile people, including her seniors, where my mother-in-law was employed.

Surprisingly, the news didn't anger me, as by now, I had thrown my wife out of my life and had made up my mind to end the relationship for each other's sake. I knew that the rust of betrayal and distrust had corroded the foundation of love and trust, and the institutions of relationships and marriage had already collapsed. And, after what I had seen with my own eyes and heard with my own ears, even if I had tried to adjust and forget everything, the marriage wouldn't have lasted long and crumbled later within a couple of years, if not months.

"Maya is just 18; she will soon get tired of waiting for me and move on to possibly better things in life," I thought to myself. She, indeed, got tired of waiting for me and getting rebuked by her mother and family repeatedly for loving and trusting me despite my repeated rebuffs. Maya stopped calling me regularly like before, though she continued to call me occasionally for some months even though I never responded, much to her continued disappointment and distress.

Almost a year passed like this, and with this, her calls stopped. "She has moved on. Maybe she has found someone better than me." I was relieved, though I didn't know why I wasn't happy with this discovery. For a few months, I continued to feel bad. However, I, too, moved on later, and soon, she was out of my thoughts; I got busy with my professional career, which had started to blossom, of late.

XII

Starting Life Anew

I joined Today's Traveller as an assistant editor. This renowned travel-based magazine was brought out by Gill India under the stewardship of Mrs. Kamal Gill—a highly respected travel writer with a defence background. In her mid-50s, she was of a relatively short height with a blotchy face, and was always smartly dressed, appropriate to her age and position.

My office was located on the second floor of a three-storey house located in Greater Kailash, an incredibly posh area of South Delhi; it offered me ample opportunities to shine in my profession and justify the high hopes of my parents. The pay package was excellent for a newcomer like me, and so were the professional prospects and opportunities.

I was only 26 at that time, and my entire life lay ahead of me. I decided to make the most of the golden opportunity that had come my way unexpectedly, to start the new chapter of my life. 'From now onwards, I will take each and every decision and step that affects my life.' Now, my movements were precise and definite; a firm purpose was evident in them. I was also determined not to repeat the silly mistakes I had committed earlier. Now, doing well in my profession was my top priority, and my personal life had taken a back seat. Getting married or starting a relationship with a new girl was out of my mind for at least a couple of years.

It's not that I and my family didn't make an effort later to restore the relationship, as we did. My parents, along with some of our relatives, went to my wife's house on at least three occasions. And though my wife's grandfather and grandmother also made genuine efforts to make the marriage work for the sake of our future and that of our families, it didn't work out mainly because Maya's mother and sisters had already made up their minds for their own reasons.

After waiting for several months, my wife's priorities had changed. She drifted away slowly constantly being egged on by her sister and mother. She had started working with a garment outlet somewhere in East Delhi with her sister, and had lost all interest in me and the life that we may have had had we not drifted apart and had the gulf between us not become unbridgeable.

When our efforts to bring her back failed, we also lost interest, and let her go to 'live' her life with freedom and ambition, the way she seemed to be interested in. I returned back to Delhi, and after a few months, I was a little delusional. Later, after a few months I got a promotion. I even had the opportunity to visit Andhra Pradesh with fellow journalists from Delhi.

On my first press tour to the southern state, I got a chance to interact and meet with some well-known journalists from some of the most reputed media houses from Delhi, including 'Hindustan Times,' 'Rashtria Sahara,' and 'Outlook Traveller.' The high point of my press tour to Andhra Pradesh was meeting the then CM of Andhra Pradesh-Mr. Chandrababu Naidu. Attired in his trademark sparklingly white shirt and trousers, the tall CM with sharp and piercing eyes welcomed the Delhi Press Team with a smile at his sprawling official address in Hyderabad. At that time, Telangana, which today has Hyderabad as its state capital, was a part of Andhra Pradesh.

Later, we had coffee with the CM while he spoke eloquently about the progress that the state had made during his tenure. He looked very alert, and had sharp, inquisitive eyes, which kept darting from one journalist to another till the time we were around with him.

After a week during which we were taken on an official tour to the different tourist attractions of the state, including Warangal, Visakhapatnam, and Hyderabad, I returned to Delhi with my fellow press people, a happy and proud person. My parents were elated and proud of me. This was just the beginning of my rapidly flourishing career. I also began to write cover stories for the prestigious Spice Route' and 'Today's Traveller magazines, with recognition pouring in for my high creativity and writing skills from far and wide.

I was in an incredibly comfortable zone; I had forgotten Maya and her family to move on to the 'bigger things of my life.' Now, like Maya and her family, I and my family had our own priorities, and we had broken away from our past and moved to a bright, positive future.

But, 'You can't live the life of celibacy after having tested the fruits of marriage'. I found it difficult to live without the company of a woman. I loved Maya and her voluptuous, soft body. I often sought solace in her warm arms and soft body and ploughed her with an unbridled and almost brutal passion, which she much loved. With her gone, I repeatedly tossed late into the night uncomfortably, with sleep eluding me completely. I frequently woke up utterly disturbed and frustrated. All sorts of negative and indescribable thoughts crossed my mind. And, I, over and over again, ended up sizing up women of 'all ages and sizes' and imagining doing indescribable things to them and having a great time with them, fulfilling my long, unfulfilled desires.

I became gloomy and terribly tired of life and everything that life threw at me. On certain occasions, my head also swam, and I ached with the fever of unrealised desire. I knew that I was badly famished, and I was fast sliding into a dangerous situation. I needed to do something urgently--without any further delays--to restore my sanity and sense of well-being. I knew that if I didn't do something fast and found an outlet for my ballooning pent-up frustrations; I would disintegrate and become rubble before long.

XIII

The End Of My Unwanted Bachelorhood

I got that outlet soon, but I would have preferred if the entire thing had been done in a better way and, importantly, with a person with whom I had been fairly comfortable and emotionally attached. After working for Gill India for close to a year, I had joined a travel and hospitality-based company in Gurgaon as a content writer.

A little fat and dark-complexioned person called Mr. Patra, ran it. He was around 55 years old and from Orissa. He was both the director and proprietor of the company, which had several properties spread across Jagannath Puri and Shimla, as well as offices in Gurugram, Delhi, and Cuttack.

Mr. Patra was a half-bald gentleman and rather peculiar in his habits. He often drank black tea in the afternoons while he ate pomegranate from a glass bowl. Other than that, he preferred to have mostly Oriya people around. So, the office had a sizeable chunk of workers with Orissa roots. However, there were some people with no links to Orissa. Apart from me, a non-native of Orissa, there were two women who were Punjabi and from Delhi.

One of them was Sheela, a voluptuous, roundly built, and fair-complexioned Punjabi woman of more or less my age. She was naturally of a gay, animated and peace-loving disposition. She was married and lived in West Patel Nagar, Delhi. She was employed as a receptionist. The first time I saw her, she was busy devouring a fast-melting ice cream during lunch hours outside the office, near a hand-driven cart. Her face appeared radiant with freshness and vigour. When she saw me looking at her intently, she broke into a wide grin, flashing her pearly white teeth, and wished me with a gentle bow of her head. She looked so positive and full of life. Unlike me, she seemed to have no complaints about life or the world.

I was fascinated. I wondered how she could be so positive and at perfect peace with the world? Her positivity and extreme love for life attracted me to her and I gradually drifted towards her. She reciprocated positively, and soon, we began exchanging glances of interest. My mind that earlier had almost choked with confusion and irritation, and my anger had also become a little calm, and my hunger for life and happiness was back.

I began to seek opportunities to talk to her whenever possible. Women have a sixth sense. She realised that I was interested in her and she gradually began to reciprocate to my overtures with infectious enthusiasm and uncontrollable laughter, making me fall in love with life all over again. I also started to drop her at the Dwarka Sector 14 Metro station on my way back home, from where she boarded the metro to reach her home in West Patel Nagar.

I felt good with her riding pillion. Her soft body teased my arms and back while my bike sped on the smooth NH-8 Delhi-Jaipur Highway and Dwarka roads. Strangely, during such times, while I often burned with desire, she looked completely at ease, as if nothing had happened. This continued for some months, during which my desire had reached its peak, and I knew that I needed to do something urgently to restore my sanity and mental equilibrium, which was almost on the verge of collapse. But I feared the likely repercussions. What if she got angry, repulsed me and informed the office management afterwards, leading to me becoming the butt of the joke among my colleagues and perhaps even getting me kicked out of my workplace?

'It's very difficult to understand women and know their innermost secrets.' Sheela had made my life hell. Though she was often pressed against my burning body for hours, riding pillion, I lacked the courage to seize the momentum and go for the kill. But, I got lucky one day, and she gave me a cue that, luckily, I made the most of by ending the sexual tension boldly and giving her an experience that brought joy to both of us in more ways than we could have imagined beforehand.

Her husband was a drunkard and had lost all appetite for the 'pleasures of life.' Sheela, thus, usually burned with desire, which she found hard to extinguish, secretively and securely. But she had realised that I was hooked and burning like her. So, after noticing my discomfort and ensuring I was the one she could trust with her deepest secrets, one day, she innocently exclaimed, "Let's go to your house and wait for some time."

Actually, it was raining heavily that day, and we got drenched badly while returning from our office. Though I stayed alone and was elated to know she wanted to spend some time with me there, I knew if I took her to my home, my neighbours might notice this. So, I was a little unsure and hesitant when she said this. But by the time we reached the Sector 14 Metro station, opposite which I lived, we were badly drenched and dripping with rainwater. Sheela, in fact, had started shivering and chattering her teeth. "A cup of hot tea would relax us, and she can change her clothes also." With this thought I brought her to my house.

Since it was raining heavily, everyone was indoors, and no one noticed that I had brought a woman to my house. Her eyes lit up when she stepped inside my one-bedroom house, located on the ground floor in a middle-class DDA locality. She soon vanished into the bathroom, and closing its door securely behind her, she changed and wiped herself dry with a small lady's towel that she had a habit of carrying. Luckily, I had some spare clothes for my wife with me that I offered her. She wore them. In my wife's clothes, she looked hot when she emerged from the bathroom after a few minutes. I became rigid with desire, all of a sudden, though unknowingly.

I was embarrassed when I found that she had noticed my 'rapidly snaking and rising discomfort.' As if to divert her attention and save myself from further embarrassment, I dashed into the kitchen hurriedly to prepare tea for her. However, she removed me instantly from there with a smile, insisting she would prepare the tea. While she was preparing the beverage, I found her singing a romantic song and turning back every two minutes to steal quick glances at me.

I knew she was on fire, like me. I also knew that if I didn't do what I was expected to do, in such an accidental and God-given situation, I would make ourselves miserable by wasting the golden opportunity that had come to perhaps both of us after a long time. So, I entered the kitchen with a nervous determination, and before I knew what I was doing, I had taken her in my arms and I was kissing her unsuspectingly, maddeningly, and fervently on her neck and cheek.

Pretending to be shocked by my unexpected behaviour, she slapped my head lightly, crying, "What the hell are you doing? Have you gone mad?" I didn't say anything but continued to kiss her ardently, like a man possessed. Her mouth and breath tasted of the vanilla ice cream that she was so fond of, and which she relished almost daily after lunch.

Soon, her resistance went away; she melted in my arms like ice cream, and her body gently opened up. Without wasting any time, I immediately brought her to the bedroom and let go of my pent-up frustrations with a frenzied passion, even though I noticed that when I was removing her clothes, my hands were shaking with excitement and nervous impatience. Sheela was equally famished and was tearing at my clothes, kissing me with almost parallel ferocity. When I finally entered her, her passion was already overflowing, and she was chewing my ears like a mouse. She was having the time of her life--perhaps after too long. And so was I.

The pace of my breaths quickened, and I began to devour her. After a while, we almost exploded together, and got transported into a different zone full of happiness and pleasure. Having spent ourselves, we lay enveloped in each other's arms and slept peacefully, like small babies, for almost two hours. Then, she suddenly got up and looked at the wall clock anxiously. "Oh, it's already 8 P.M.! I must hurry and leave without any delays!" She cried, a little alarmed.

When I dropped her later, the rain had stopped pelting the world, and everything looked so fresh and soothing green. All the nearby trees and shrubs looked welcoming, drenched with the happiness and colours of life. This time around, I hadn't dropped her off at the Sector 14 Metro station but at her place, which was about seven kilometres away from my place. When she got down from my coal-black 180 CC Pulsar bike, she held my hand tightly and whispered in my ears, "I love you." Then, she quickly melted into the surging evening market crowd of shoppers and hawkers, and even before I could say anything or react, she vanished.

I returned home a completely changed person. I had a smile and a spring in my feet. I was on cloud 9. The world had suddenly become a nice place for me. The acute darkness of frustration and bitterness had vanished, and a beautiful, bright, and vibrant rainbow of life shone in all its luminosity before my eyes. It brimmed with happiness after a long time.

With Sheela around, how days passed quickly, I don't remember. Every day, I gave her a lift while returning, and she clung to me like a reed while my motorcycle sped towards its destination. Our growing proximity hadn't gone unobserved, and there were whispers around and all-knowing smiles thrown at us every now and then by our smiling colleagues and common friends who seemed to be jealous of me. "Bastard, he is so lucky; he must be having lots of fun!" But we were least bothered and continued to seek solace and happiness in each other's arms.

After about two months, she suddenly stopped coming to the office. I was a miserable man. I reached out to her only to learn that she had lost her husband. Strangely, she didn't seem distraught on the phone; she appeared calm and in full control of the situation. She rejoined the office after a couple of days. And, we were back to our old ways, discovering life and each other's deepest secrets together. Life was good, and we began to have a wonerful time again.

Sheela had filled the void left by my wife, and I hardly missed the person whom I once loved the most in the world. But as they say, "Good times don't last long," one day I received a call from home that disrupted my life in a big way, and I was back to the darkest phases of my life.

Part IV

XIV
The Death of Ma

"Ma is no more; she died early in the morning." It was around 10:20 AM and my elder sister was on the line. It was a clear, wintry morning. I had just reached my workplace in Gurgaon and was busy dusting my desk and laptop. Then she broke down, and I couldn't figure out what she was saying.

It was in the month of December 2008--the year of the Mumbai attack. Just about a fortnight ago, there had been an attack on Mumbai by some Islamist terrorists, who had poured in, undetected, from across the borders. A large number of people had lost their lives in 10+ perfectly synchronised shooting and bombing attacks across India's financial capital. The entire country was furious, and Indo-Pak relations had deteriorated to an all-time low.

Strangely, I didn't cry. However, I had turned white and was gasping for breath as the news had not sunk in yet. It had left me numb, though, and my brain had difficulty processing the information and figuring-out what had actually happened. I wasn't ready to accept that the person around whom my entire world revolved was no more.

"How could this be possible? How could Ma go away suddenly like this? Do mothers leave quietly like this? She has cheated me!" I was furious and mad, with an impotent rage and confusion. I looked at myself as if I were seeking an answer from someone. There was no one around me.

I returned to my thoughts. "Who gave the old woman the right to die like this? What she thinks of herself...Selfish woman...she died without even thinking once about her kids..." Now, my eyes had welled up, but I wasn't crying.

My sister--who by now had somewhat regained her composure—clearing her throat, added, "She died in the hospital where we had admitted her a week ago." She paused for some time as if waiting for my reaction, and when there was none, she choked again as she had by now understood that I wasn't in a position to talk and was battling against the same sea of emotions and trying to grapple with the same situation plaguing her. She disconnected when I didn't respond despite her many attempts to connect.

After some time, I sat down quietly on a chair nearby and sat there motionless for almost half an hour, lost in deep thought. While I sat frozen, lost in my thoughts and muttering all sorts of weird things about Ma in anger and depression, I suddenly noticed someone standing near me and looking intently at my face. It was Harpreet, the HR Manager.

Looking inquisitively and steadily at my face, which by now had twitched convulsively, she offered me a glass of water. Afterwards, bringing her face remarkably close to my face and putting her left hand gently on my right shoulder, she asked, "What happened?" By now she had figured out that some calamity had befallen me all of a sudden and left me shattered.

I didn't say anything and continued to remain quiet and motionless. She repeated her question, this time around a bit loudly. This broke my reverie. Looking at her worried face, I articulated almost in a whisper, "Ma is no more." She looked at me, a little confused. By now, Sheela had arrived on the scene. She became a little curious when she found me in such a state and Harpreet huddled close to me. She wondered what was happening. When she leanred that something had struck me powerfully, she, like Harpreet, came closer and then, and then taking my hand in her hand, sympathetically asked me what had happened.

I, who so far had been battling with my emotions and grief for almost an hour, suddenly started crying. Tears began to flow freely. Soon, my cheeks and the white shirt that I had worn got drenched with my tears. This further alarmed the two women; they looked at each other for a moment, wondering what to do and how to comfort me in such a difficult situation.

By then a few of my other office colleagues, going out for lunch, had arrived on the scene. On learning what the matter was they immediately swung into action. While one kind soul arranged a plane ticket for me, another called a taxi for me right away. I left several worried faces after half an hour or so and reached the city airport within 40-45 minutes. There, after waiting for a few hours, and completing the airport formalities before taking my boarding pass, I boarded the Patna-bound SpiceJet Airlines sometime around 5 PM in the evening.

I was a changed person now. I knew that from now onwards the world won't be the same place for me without Ma around. While the going away of my wife had disrupted my life and disturbed me badly, the unexpected and sudden loss of my Ma had turned my whole world upside down and snuffed out the flickering flame of whatever little happiness that still remained in my life.

Ma's unexpected death had completely unhinged me, and I lay prostrate at the feet and the mercy of insurmountable and endless grief. Ma was the one I looked to every time I had some issues in my life, and I sought the comforting presence of the person I was closest to. With her gone, who would I call every time to help me get out of the chaos and get my life back on track?

"Ma, I will never forgive you...but I am happy that you died so unexpectedly and so early...because selfless people like you have no right to live and get old in this world... all your life, you didn't spend a single penny on yourself and thought only about your family and kids...you deserved to die like this." I swore under my breath. Suddenly, my plane heaved and began running with a deafening sound and lightning speed. Soon, it left the runway and became airborne.

When I reached Patna around 6:30, it had already become a little dark, and the city shone bright with the lights of commercials and billboards of all kinds. It was my first journey by air. All through the one-and-a-half-hour journey from Delhi to Patna, I remained in a state of unease, wondering what to do next and how to survive in the world that didn't anymore have the comforting presence of Ma. When the smiling air hostess of the plane, decked up in the trademark colourful bright outfits, asked me if I would like to have something, I didn't say anything and continued to look a distance away--vaguely and without a purpose. She left hurriedly, thinking I wasn't in the mood to have anything.

When I eventually reached my house around 7:30 P.M., I was greeted by a sea of relatives and neighbours. My entire house resembled a graveyard with not a single soul smiling or behaving in their usual way. Ma was very popular in the area and everyone loved and respected her. Her unexpected and sudden death had shaken the entire community and neighbourhood and plunged them into the sea of grief.

As soon as my two sisters saw me, they rushed to me and then started wailing loudly. I, who had worn a stony silence till until then and had withheld my tears with resilience, gave in and broke down immediately. My eyes welled up, and soon, I was howling like a small baby. My sudden outpouring of grief in such a moving way caught the attention of everyone, including my weeping sisters; they looked at me, confused and alarmed, wondering how to react and what to do in such a situation.

I don't remember for how long I kept on crying like this. But I do remember that when I suddenly found my head reeling and when I was about to almost fall, one of my maternal uncles quickly stepped forward, and gently holding my swaying body, he helped me settle down on a nearby chair. Then, gently wiping my tears with a grey cotton towel with white flowers carved on it, he asked a person standing close by to fetch him a glass of water fast. Then, after offering me the water promptly, he began rebuking my (now quiet) sisters for such a strong display of grief and emotions.

Soon an air of sanity descended quietly on all those around. Our relatives started making preparations to ferry Ma to the place located on the banks of the Ganga, where the final journey of most of the people in our community ends. A huge pier of wood was erected near the banks of the river and several kilos of clarified butter were put on it.

Then, a dark-skinned and semi-naked dom (untouchables due to their role in disposing of bodies, including both human and animal remains), handed over a burning wooden pole to me. I set the pier-- on which Ma lay peacefully and serenely, with her arms crossed and pressed on her boson, as though carved out of marble--to fire.

She had a bindi on her forehead and her head was smeared with sindoor. While she was alive, her worst fear was to die as a widow. I remember when once she had shown her palm to a jyotish (astrologer) in Delhi, she had asked him if she would die a married woman. The smiling jyotish had asked, "What do you want?" "I want to die as a married woman." She has returned quickly. He had told her that wish would be fulfilled as this was what the future had in store for her.

Ma was a religious and spiritual person. Perhaps this is why God had fulfilled her wish, and she had died a married woman with her husband around. But she was selfish in the sense that she hadn't thought of my poor father and visualised what would happen to this simple ex-army man, who, all his life, had remained very close to her and who didn't do any single thing without consulting her. He was so used to her having around that with her sudden death, his entire world had come crashing down, and he had lost the will to live. He regularly lay awake till late into the night and wailed inconsolably. At such times, he also cursed God for snatching his partner for life. He also often talked to Lord Hanuman (he was a devoted Hanuman bhakt) and asked him when he would end his miseries and help him meet Ma in the other world.

It was heartbreaking to see such a strong military man who had lived his life with dignity, with his head high and crying like a child. It was heart-wrenching for all of us. Deep inside, we all knew that he wouldn't survive for long in such a painful condition, though we prayed to God to keep him healthy and happy, for as long as possible. After the sudden death of Ma, we weren't prepared to face another huge blow. Still, I found it difficult to watch him crumble under the weight of his mounting grief and degenerate physically and mentally with every passing day.

After spending roughly 20 days and completing all the rituals related to Ma's death, I returned to Delhi. When, after about a month, I returned to Patna, I was shocked to see my father in such an incredibly dangerous condition. He had not only lost over 20 kilograms in just about a month, he also looked almost like a corpse with no visible signs of life left in his sunken eyes that once glowed with happiness and life.

When I touched his feet and sought his blessings, he didn't recognise me for some minutes; he remained motionless and expressionless, looking at me with a vacant and vague expression. And when he finally recognized me, having aroused himself from his stupor with some difficulty, he immediately burst into tears and started crying like a child. This shook me completely, and I at once made up my mind to take him to Delhi, nurse him back to health, and bring back his lost appetite for life.

"I can't lose him; he must survive for at least the next 10-15 years and play with his grandchildren, my kids," I murmured. When Ma was alive, she desperately wanted to see my kids. It was her wish, and I was determined to fulfil that wish by presenting my father with my kids, with whom he could play and derive joy. I returned to Delhi after about a week intending to rent a bigger house there and return to my native place after a fortnight to take my father back with me.

It was a big mistake; I shouldn't have left him alone in such a state. I regretted my decision for long.

XV

The Death of My Father

The year 2011 was remarkable in many ways. That year, Anna Hazare, the veteran socialist and champion of those marginalised-much disillusioned with the all-pervasive corruption and the sorry state of affairs in the nation during the Congress rule, both at the Centre and across many states of India under the ruling party, undertook fast for Jan Lokpal Bill at Jantar Manta, in New Delhi. Several top personalities, including Kiran Bedi, Arvind Kejriwal, and Aamir Khan, lent their support to the movement, which also drew large crowds of students and common people from far and wide. The air in Delhi was thick with hope—that of a corruption-free India and everyone seemed to be buoyed with the prospects of a better tomorrow under the leadership of the modern Gandhi, i.e., Anna Hazare.

The year was notable in the country's history for yet another important development. India beat Sri Lanka in the finals to win the prestigious Cricket World Cup under the captaincy of MS Dhoni, who scored 91 (not out) in the most important match of the tournament and emerged as the 'Player of the Match.' The entire city and the country erupted with joy and chants of 'Bharat Mata Ki Jai' rent the air even while sweets were freely distributed by the overjoyed and dancing cricket fans and others.

But, the year is etched in my memory for another (more) important reason: I lost my father that year. I still remember that just four days after returning to Delhi and visiting my dangerously upset father, I received a call from Didi. It was in 2011, in the month of February. For some vague reasons, my heart shook with trepidation. "Hope everything is fine with Pa," I murmured. All sorts of negative thoughts came rushing fast to me, though.

My worst thoughts had come true. "Pa is no more; he died peacefully in his sleep this morning," I heard the familiar voice of Didi. This time around, strangely, she was quiet and composed. She had, perhaps, steeled her nerves, or maybe her tears had dried by now. She knew that with Pa also gone, she was the one who had to take charge of the family with maturity and full responsibility.

I rushed to Patna the next day by the morning train and stayed there for a fortnight, during which I underwent the same heart-wrenching experience that I had experienced just two years ago. My relatives had put him on a thick slab of ice to stop his dead body from decomposing. When he was alive, Papa was a rather tall and extremely well-built, and fair man; in death, his body looked shrunk and a pale shadow of what he was earlier.

After performing the death rituals, feeding pundits, and performing the pind daan (a Hindu ritual carried out to pay homage and offer prayers to late ancestors), with a heavy heart, I boarded Sampoorna Kranti for Delhi, leaving the place where my Ma and Papa had spent their lives, and where I had spent the most memorable period of my life with them. As I was the youngest child of my parents, I was pampered and loved the most by them. With Papa also gone, my umbilical attachment to the place had broken, and it haunted me with memories of a bygone era. While boarding the train to Delhi, I looked at the railway station with sad eyes and a pained soul.

I knew that with Papa and Ma no more, the place wouldn't be same for me anymore, and perhaps only after a long time would I return to the city again. When the train finally groaned, heaved, and, with a jerk, began to move slowly, I came out of my reverie. I looked outside through the iron window, to cast a sweeping look at the platform. By then, the train had gained speed, and everything on the platform seemed to become blurred and distorted. With tears, I bid adieu to the place that I loved so much and that once ruled my heart.

With the death of Papa, my life went off-track again in a big way, and I lay exposed to the mercy of the world unprotected and unsheltered. How I spent my days in a vacuum for a long time, I have only a hazy recollection. For several days at the end, I remained almost confined to my house, and didn't venture out much. I also didn't rejoin my office despite receiving many calls from my boss and friends.

Through this most difficult and taxing phase of life, I also learnt that my wife had filed for divorce. But, strangely, the news didn't trouble me as I had braced myself mentally for it. It was inevitable. The relationship had been dead for a long time, and it was better to part ways legally for each other's sake. I consulted with my lawyer. She advised me to part ways mutually, at the Dwarka Family Court, where my wife had filed the case for the annulment of the marriage.

When I went to court on the day fixed for our first appearance before the magistrate, I was a little surprised to see my wife in an entirely different avatar. She was attired in the latest fashionable clothes. She looked entirely different. She had gained a lot of weight and appeared bloated. Other than her weight, what surprised me the most was her behaviour. See seemed betrayed and angry with me, though I had difficulty figuring out why. It perplexed me why, when she had filed for divorce, and I had responded positively to the matter that she had wanted, she didn't seem pleased.

Was she thinking that with maturity and patience, I would make some efforts to salvage the wreckage that our relationship had become? Was she still thinking that everything would become normal, like before? I have no idea, as I was highly dustrubed. I quietly did what I was advised to do by my lawyer--a somewhat beautiful and fair-complexioned young woman from the North East in her early 30s who lived in the same place where I lived and who seemed to be a rather good person. She advised me to do what was expected by my wife and her lawyer, to save myself from the barrage of legal cases that they had filed against me.

At the Dwarka District Court, I learned through my counsel that my wife had filed dowry and domestic violence cases against me at the Tis Hazari Court, apart from the divorce case that they had already filed at the Dwarka District Court. If I hadn't agreed to her counsel's request for mutual divorce, they would have left no stone unturned to get me behind bars. I knew that the Indian judicial system is heavily biased in favour of women, and men can be put behind bars on even flimsy, baseless grounds.

The divorce led to severed lives, ending the chapter forever, though it also simultaneously opened new avenues for both. Soon after my divorce my maternal aunts and others from my family flooded me with calls and messages. They wanted me to get married to the girl of their choice. They assumed that since I was legally single, they had the right to get me married to the girl of their choice. And so they began arranging for suitable brides for me and made me visit them on one pretext or the other so that they could fix up a meeting with the 'nice' girls on their radar.

Though I wasn't too willing and mentally prepared to start afresh so soon, as the bitterness of my breakup still lingered, I began visiting them when the pressure became unbearable and I started meeting the girls arranged by them, one after another, sometimes at the local temple and sometimes at some other public places, like the market.

However, since I was still in a rather agitated and confused state of mind, and deep inside knew that marriage wouldn't work for me, I remained uninterested and indecisive, with a dogged indifference. As a result, when I gave no concrete response, after some time, they became weary, and their enthusiasm to 'settle me' fizzled out. They abandoned all their plans, and I was back at the mercy of my disturbed and unhinged thoughts, wondering what to do next, or how to seize back control of my life that had become rudderless and devoid of any purpose, post the twin deaths of Ma and Papa one after another in quick successions, and the painful separation from my former wife.

XVI

The Abyss of Moral Degeneration

After the death of my father, I had stopped doing a job because I didn't have the inspiration for it anymore. Doing well in my chosen profession--for which I had the necessary degrees and for which my parents had spent their hard-earned money--wasn't something that excited or inspired me any longer, as my parents were no more. But since I had to do something productive to make both ends meet and keep myself busy, I drifted towards 'things' and people unknowingly and unintentionally--my parents certainly wouldn't have approved of them had they been alive.

While I was in such an unstable state of mind, floating in the waters of vagueness and de-motivation, and wondering what to do next, I came across one property dealer named Shyam Sunder Vohra, who had his office in a Bakkarwala, Najafgarh—the birthplace and village of the former Chief Minister of Delhi, Late Sahib Singh Verma. After the death of Ma, I had sold off my Dwarka flat and bought a one-bedroom flat in Loknayak Puram, Bakkarwala—a sleepy and somewhat cut-off dusty settlement located in the semi-rural area of Najafgarh, on the outskirts of Dwarka, near Nangloi.

During those days, Loknayak Puram had six DDA pockets with 1000s of small-sized LIG flats.

I don't know why I sold off my one bedroom flat located in a posh and developed area such as Dwarka, bang opposite the Sector 14 Metro station, to move to a backward and cut-off area, with not even proper roads. However, this is what I did, and I regretted my decision for a long time, not because it brought my downfall and destruction in more ways than I can remember, but also because the decision changed my entire life for the worse. And, I plunged head down—like a professional diver into the deep, bottomless waters of debauchery and moral bankruptcy, not to mention HUGE financial losses, from which I couldn't recover for long.

At my new place of abode, the ground floor flat located opposite the central park of the DDA Pocket to which I had moved, Mr Vohra, a fat Punjabi man of medium height and a spotty face, was my neighbour. I still remember that the first time I saw him, it was around 8 AM in the morning, and he was polishing his leather shoes while sitting in front of his ground floor house-cum-office. When our eyes met, he greeted me with a broad smile.

He had learned from somebody that I was from Dwarka and that I had recently purchased a flat in his locality. He also had some idea about my financial standing and perhaps knew that I had some decent money in my banks. He also perhaps knew that I was an 'unhinged' and 'directionless' person who had lost his parents, one by one, in quick succession recently.

Being a creepy fellow, and sensing a good opportunity to make some quick money, he began luring me with all sorts of temptations. He was interested in the money that I had, thanks to my properly planned investments in Dwarka and my father's and mother's generous contributions to my financial resources, by way of Post Office and bank deposits that they had done for me over the years.

Over a period of time, he also learnt that I had recently divorced my former wife, and the separation had unhinged me completely, creating a big void in my already unhinged life. So, with a pre-planned motive, he introduced me to several usual temptations of life that promised quick salvations and relief from my mental agony and emotional void.

Though I had a feeling that what I was doing wasn't morally right, being weak in the flesh, like most mortals, I soon became prey to his sinister motives, and before long, I began to slip down on the greasy pole of moral degenerations and financial losses. By the time I could figure out what was really happening and where I was heading without any breaks or checks, I had lost everything; I had nothing, money nor mental peace.

Egged on by Vohra--who often welcomed me with steaming chicken curry prepared in ghee, and delicious sweets bought from a famous sweet shop located near Dwarka Modh--I began meeting girls and women of dubious characters, arranged by him, one by one. I also started investing huge sums of money and loaning huge amounts to him, as he made me believe that I would get handsome 'returns' soon, thanks to the ongoing property boom in the area. During those days, the work on the proposed highway that connects Gurgaon and the NH-8 with Nangloi and other similar areas located near Bakkarwala was in full flow, and there was a lot of speculation about the likely spiralling property prices in the areas across Bakkarwala and the adjoining regions.

Milking the momentum with the prospects of a boom, he ensnared me and convinced me to start making investments and make lots of money, within a short period of time. In the beginning, I was a little hesitant and evasive. When he noticed that I wasn't convinced, he disarmed me, saying, "Make small investments; only after you get good returns on your investments, go for big investments. Trust me;

you will make lots of money within a short period of time!"

This disarmed me, and I made a starting investment of one lakh rupees, hoping to test the waters first. He returned the money exactly after the pre-decided period of three months with a profit of 30 K. A profit of 30 K on an investment of just one lakh rupees within just three months excited me and sent a surge of happiness through my body.

When on the next day of receiving my principal amount with interest, he asked me to invest more, to earn more, I agreed at once. This time around, the investment that I had made was huge. The amount was Rs four lakhs, and the promised profit on my principal amount was Rs. 12, 0000 in just three months. On the due date, I received my principal amount with the promised profit like before. I was elated. Blinded by the lure of easy money, I began to invest more from then onwards. Little did I know, or had an idea that I was getting sucked into something from where it would be difficult for me to return later unscathed.

With time, the principal amount kept heading north, and so was the profit. Then came a time when he began to stress that it wasn't wise to take the invested principal amounts so soon, as I was letting go of bigger returns. He convinced me that I should re-invest my principal amounts for bigger returns on my investments. By then, I had become so enchanted and blinded by tempting returns that I agreed without any hesitation and stopped looking forward to receiving my principal amounts. My entire attention and focus had shifted to the expected returns. I had completely overlooked the fact that he was only returning small amounts of my own money, to keep me happy and satisfied.

This continued for almost a year, during which I invested close to 35 lakh. It was a significant amount at that time. When I checked my bank accounts one day, I learned that I had just 1, 50000/- rupees left in my two accounts. I was shocked. Sensing something seriously wrong with my method of earning money, I spoke with a chartered accountant known to me, and sought her advice.

XVII
The Awakening

"Am I doing the right thing by making such kinds of investments?" I asked her one day, after having shared with her everything related to the matter with her, when I visited her at her office, tucked away in the corner of a narrow, dusty lane of Vikaspuri in West Delhi.

It was around 9:30 in the morning, and the daylight was streaming in through the windows of her first-floor office, which overlooked a dirty drain that ended abruptly somewhere near the entrance of a shop stuffed with kids' toys. The accountant, a married woman around 35 years old with a somewhat flat nose from Uttarakhand, looked strangely at me for some time. Then, still looking at me with the same expression, she asked me, "How old are you?" I was a little taken aback by her strange question. When I replied a little uneasily that I was around 32, she looked at me with almost the same expression. This time around, I could detect a hint of mockery in her eyes.

"Do you have any idea what the hell are you doing?" She asked me, throwing a drowsy and indifferent glance at me now. On getting no response from me, she added, "You have been foolishly and recklessly investing money with a person who I am sure won't return your money now."

By now, panic had gripped me. Trembling from inside with an unknown fear, I asked her what made her think so. "Well, as I can understand, you have been giving money to a property dealer, expecting handsome returns soon. But now almost six months have gone by, and you haven't received your principal amounts. It means this gentleman has grabbed your money, and he has no intentions to return it."

Then, looking at me with a fixed stare, she added, "But I find it a little difficult to understand why you kept on giving him money for so long without first getting your principal amounts back." By now, she looked a little doubtful and not very sure if I had really given such a big amount to Vohra.

I didn't say anything and returned home disillusioned and tired late in the afternoon. "How could I be such an asshole and give my hard-earned money to this bastard?" I was angry with myself and kept cursing all the way through my return journey. I was both aghast and distressed in equal measures and felt stupid with my own inexplicable and foolish actions.

The very next day, plunged in deep thought, I went to Vohra's place, excited. After exchanging the usual pleasantries with him, I asked him politely but firmly to start returning the principal amounts that I had given to him over the course of the past year. "I require money badly as I have some very important tasks at hand that I need to do on a priority basis," I said, looking at him intently but distrustfully.

He didn't respond, though he looked visibly unhappy and irritated. He remained silent for some time, studying me as if he were wondering what to say and how to face sudden, unexpected situations. Then, clearing his throat and looking at the white ceiling of his real estate office, he said, "Why are you in a hurry to stop your investments? You are doing so well. Handsome returns are just around the corner. So please have some patience."

I glanced at him mistrustfully and angrily. By now, it was clear that he had no intentions to return my money as he, perhaps, had none, having already spent it on a brand new car and some expensive household items, such as a refrigerator, washing machine, designer furniture, AC, LCD, etc., that I had noticed he had bought recently. Even though I was furious and agitated with him and his replies, for some unknown reason, I didn't press the matter further. I returned home with the intention of thinking over the matter thoroughly and taking expert advice from a professional on the matter.

Soon, I spoke with some lawyers at the Dwarka District Court and sought their advice. After minutely examining the agreements signed between Vohra and me and the cheques issued by him against the principal amounts that I had given him, they asked me to start depositing the cheques. "We will drag him to the court and file both criminal and civil cases if the cheques go dishonoured, as they are likely to be, given the current state of affairs and his reluctance to pay. When the law enforcement agencies tighten their noose around his neck, he will have no options except to return all the money that he has taken on the pretext of investments back to you."

I returned home that day, much relieved and very happy. In the meantime, sensing the likely trouble from my side, Vohra began to 'distract' me even more and more with the dubious contacts that he had, and I, who should by now have resolutely stayed away from him and his people, strangely, almost lost track of my goal and began to eat out of his hands yet again. Much to my horror, I gradually became a wretched slave to my own desire and began to seek more happiness and pleasures from every possible wrong place and from all sorts of wrong people, while the eternally henna-dyed Punjabi with a bloated face and a throaty voice continued to push me further down the abyss of no return.

However, when I regained my mental equilibrium after some time, I asked him again to return my money one day. But, predictably, Vohra didn't respond positively. Seething with anger, I decided to take things under my control in a way for which he had, perhaps, already braced himself up by now. He knew that one day the situation would deteriorate and I would be at his throat. So, he had fortified his defenses, and created a situation for which I had neither anticipated nor was prepared, as I had almost no idea about what the future held for me and how he would backstab me in such a way.

It all began with me one evening in the month of October, landing at his place unannounced and asking him firmly and decisively to return my principal amounts within a week. It was a windy afternoon, and the wind was howling with all its raw energy and unspent ferocity. I had a tough time driving my bike on the potholed and broken road that took me to his place. When I expressed my desire to get my money back after I sat down on a chair kept opposite his desk behind, I found him seated comfortably, having tea from a huge coffee mug. For a couple of moments, he didn't reply. Afterwards, putting aside his empty mug, he began to give me incoherent and vague explanations. "You would soon get handsome returns; it's just a question of a few months'.'

However, by now, my patience had run thin as I hadn't only become suspicious of him and his motives, but I also had a genuine need for money as I was planning to shift back to Dwarka and start my life afresh, reconstructing it step-by-step and bringing it to its former glory. What had further stirred me to distance myself from the likes of Vohra was that I had recently received a nice job offer from a Nehru Place-based immigration consultancy for the post of senior content writer.

The new job promised good remuneration, coupled with other

perks that come with such a position. It also meant that I would be able to justify (though a little delayed) my high educational qualifications and upbringing, for which my deceased parents had spared no effort and made big sacrifices while they were alive. I had made up my mind to grab the opportunity that I believed would not only restore sanity to my life and some much-needed money in my account but also help me free myself from his vicious clutches. Besides, I also didn't like the backward and crime-infested place that Bakkarwala was, having spent most of my earlier years in the various developed and respected areas of Dwarka and elsewhere.

When he didn't respond in the manner that I wanted and continued to give incoherent and vague explanations, I suddenly lost my cool and yelled at him in a businesslike, dry, and even contemptuous, menacing tone, "Either pay what's due to me or face the consequences." Afterwards, throwing a malicious glance at him, I stomped out of his office purposefully. I was violently excited and determined to put him down and set him in his proper place.

He didn't say anything that day, but when I barged into his office the next day in the same way, dripping with uncontrolled rage and passion, and asked him to pay right away, he immediately called some people, who, I later learned, were local pehelwans and goons. In the surrounding semi-rural areas of Bakkarwala, there is no dearth of such people who specialise in intimidating people with their raw muscle power to persuade them to do what is required by those who pay them. But by the time they arrived at his place, I had already left with the intention to return again.

I later learned from a source that Vohra was planning to get me manhandled and beaten severely, so that I got terrified and lost interest in the recovery of my money. Now, the situation had spiralled out of control; I had to move ahead with maturity as I was entirely alone in the area and had to recover my money without getting myself physically harmed in any manner.

The next day, I shared my problem with some of my well-wishers, one of whom advised me to sell my Bakkarwala flat and buy another flat with that money in Dwarka and move to it fast. They also said, "Don't visit Vohra hoping to get your money back; he will get you manhandled."

I did as advised, as by now, I had realised that some untoward event was just around the corner, and so I needed to act very fast to get back to a safe and respectable situation away from the reach of Vohra and his notorious contacts. After disposing-off my ground-floor flat in Bakkarwala quickly, at a throw-away price, to a foul-smelling, kohl-eyed Sardar from West Patel Nagar, I bought a second-floor, ill-kempt DDA flat in Dwarka and moved to it without any further delays. To be on the safer side, I also ensured that Vohra didn't get a hint of what I had done or where I had swiftly moved.

After I had shifted to my new place hurriedly, I heaved a sigh of relief. Since no one knew where I had moved to after moving out of Bakkarwala, I felt quite safe and secure. Thanks to my speedy exit from Bakkarwala, I also managed to keep the women and other similar shady characters from his circle away after my showdown with Vohra that day. They started making frantic efforts to blackmail me and threaten me with dire consequences if I didn't back off, and I didn't stop making efforts to make him pay.

Having secured my well-being and safety and moved back to my familiar and comfortable environments, I moved on to my next course of action of going on an offensive, legally. I contacted some lawyers from the nearby Dwarka District Court and shared my issue with them. I learned that since I had many cheques issued by Vohra with me, I should start depositing them on the due dates, and if they bounced (as was the likelihood), I should file criminal and civil cases against him for the legal recovery of the pending amounts.

"Don't worry; you will get your money back with full interest," said Mr. Chhabra, a senior lawyer with a sharp face and a protruding nose. Just pay me Rs. one lakh in the beginning and 5000 rupees at every successive court appearance, and leave the rest to me. I will put the fear of God in this Punjabi," he said with a decisive tone, studying my agitated and excited face.

He looked 50 or older and had patches of gray hair on his strange-looking head. Overall, he looked rather knowledgeable and experienced. After thinking over the matter for a couple of minutes, during which I kept on drinking the endless cups of cardamom-flavoured tea offered by Mr. Chhabra and looking at his chamber, lined with thick volumes of law books, I decided to follow his advice.

I withdrew the amount from the bank located inside the court premises, and then I quietly gave it to him. Then, after filling in the vakalatnama that he fished out from his overflowing drawer, I left his 6th-floor lawyers' chambers on a somewhat buoyant note, believing that I would soon receive my lost money back. At that time, I didn't know or understand how the legal system worked in India, and I was getting sucked into yet another hopeless and bad situation. I also had no idea that legal cases dragged on for decades in our country, and it was the plaintiffs, or the ones who had filed the cases, who got prosecuted and fleeced in most of the cases by the courts and the lawyers.

By the time I realised this, it was too late again. I had not only lost whatever little money I had been able to make, thanks to my new job, but also wasted several precious years of my productive life running from one court to another for the recovery of my hard-earned money. All that I got from the courts was long, extended dates for the next court hearings, sometimes running into six months.

Tareekh pe Tareekh...

Since Vohra had my money, he used it cleverly against me to keep the cases dragging on for years by hiring some of the best and most battle-hardened lawyers, who kept on proving before the magistrates sitting a little bored behind huge shining desks, that he wasn't accountable to pay a single penny to me as it was me who was responsible for the mess. It was I who had made unplanned and ill-thought-out investments without thinking about the accompanying market risks.

All through this long, painful phase of my life--stretching to almost seven years of my life that saw me making countless fruitless court appearances and paying hefty fees to my different lawyers of varied experiences, I lost not only close to six lakh rupees but also the will to fight against Vohra in the courts. "It's high time for another 'pause' and 'reset' in my life, to restore some sanity back in my life and salvage what little I have still been left with," I muttered aloud while returning from the court later that day, ignoring the reactions of some of the startled pedestrians who looked at me a little confused.

When I reached my house in the evening, completely weary and exhausted after having wasted yet another day at the so-called Temple of Justice, darkness had already descended, and the new moon was shining brightly upon my face. It seemed pleased with my latest decision. Soon after taking a cold shower and washing two stale parathas down my hungry throat with a mug of tea, I retired to my bed, a little calm and satisfied with the new decision.

I had a strange dream, though, that night. I saw myself grappling with Vohra and his wrestler goons in a muddy field and getting severely beaten by them. I awoke the next day late in the morning, when the sun had already begun to shine high up in the sky and was visible from my window, throwing its dazzling lights all around and bathing the glass panes of my first-floor accommodation with its blinding rays. My head was aching badly, and I even felt a little feverish and low on energy.

After freshening up and having a hurried cup of ginger-flavoured tea, I left for my office. "Today also, I am late. I wonder what my boss would think of me." I muttered while driving my bike to my office. During those days, I was working for an Okhla-based marketing and communication agency as a copywriter.

Fortunately, when I reached my office, my boss--a dark-skinned, extremely ambitious Malayalee in his early 40s--had still not turned up. And so, moving stealthily and hurriedly to my desk, ignoring the questioning look of the tall receptionist who was writing something in a register spread before her, I immediately began working unnoticed and undetected by most others, without the fear of getting severely reprimanded by my boss for my late arrival.

Of late, I had been arriving late at my office almost every second or third day due to my disturbed state of mind and endless court proceedings. For my lateness, he had reprimanded me on at least three occasions earlier.

XVIII
Yet Another Death

One major reason behind my decision to discontinue the court cases was Mr. Kanishka Gupta, who had always strongly advised me to live life in a positive way away from all kinds of shady people and all sorts of legal encumbrances. He was my senior in media and an extremely nice person. The first time I met him was in Gill, India, where I had my first job.

I was employed by Gill India as an assistant editor at Greater Kailash. During those days, the publishing group, which was composed of a 45-plus go-getting Punjabi woman, Mrs. Kamal Gill, brought out a couple of magazines for its clients. Today's Traveller (a well-known travel and hospitality-based monthly) and SpiceRoute (the in-flight magazine of SpiceJet Airlines) were two such names.

Mr. Gupta had joined the publishing group as its chief editor. At that time, while he was around 38 years old, I was around 28 years old. He had amazing writing, editing, and story-telling skills, and did a decent job with the publications, giving them a new direction that soon began to fetch the management good revenues from their various clients, including SpiceJet Airlines, for which Gill India published SpiceRoute.

Mr. Gupta was half-bald and a little dark in complexion. He was rather odd in his ideas. He was a chain smoker and smoked at least 6 to 10 cigarettes a day. He was from Gwalior and stayed in a rented apartment in Mayur Vihar with his family. He was not a man who was easy to draw out; he mostly remained confined to his world and preferred his own company to that of others. This somewhat alienated him from others working there.

He, however, was fairly comfortable with me and enjoyed my company. We often went out together for lunch and tea breaks. While I respected him for his professional skills and vast experience in the field, he liked me for the fresh approach that I had to writing. He frequently praised me before others and even got me a salary hike of Rs 1000 (a princely amount during those days) from the management.

He was a little moody and had strong personal views about things and people. If he found something or some people not to his liking, he expressed his disapproval and dislike openly. While I hardly took notice of all his peculiarities and eccentricities, others around weren't magnanimous. So, he didn't have any friends in Gill, India. In fact, before long, he had many 'secret' enemies who joined hands to get him out of the office. They poisoned the management's ears against him and levelled him as unfriendly, disruptive, and not a team player.

They claimed that he wasn't only arrogant, but he also had a habit of throwing his weight around in the office, and he repeatedly treated his juniors harshly, though this wasn't true. Actually, the entire game had been played by one Malayalee woman, Radhika, who was next to him in seniority. She wasn't comfortable with the newcomer, Mr. Gupta, being put in charge of the group above her. So, she poisoned the management's ears against him. She planned her move carefully and used his aloofness and unfriendliness in the office against him to turn everyone, barring me, against him. She created such a hostile and unfriendly atmosphere against him that Mr. Gupta, in a fit of anger, hastily resigned from his post one day. I was on leave that day.

However, when he realised his mistake later and understood how Radhika had played her cards against him to get him out of Gill India, he sent an e-mail to the management expressing his desire to take his resignation back and rejoin the office. A little confused, Mrs. Gill sought our views, and predictably, everyone sided with Radhika. This scuttled Mr. Gupta's chance of rejoining Gill India.

After Mr. Gupta's unceremonious exit, I hadn't heard from him for a couple of years. I had almost forgotten him when, one day early in the morning, he called me and asked where I was and how I was doing. By then, I had also moved out of Gill, India, and had started working with an Astrology-based organisation called Astroyogi in Vasant Kunj, run by a fat woman in her early 50s. He turned up the very next day to meet me there; we became close again and began sharing many memorable moments over endless cups of tea and bread pakoras. We began to meet at all possible places where we were comfortable, including Connaught Place, Rajouri Garden, Vasant Kunj, Greater Kailash, and Nehru Place.

We are mostly at some central place in the city, like Connaught Place, located almost equidistant from Mayur Vihar and Dwarka, where we lived in that order. He was a big devotee of Lord Hanuman Ji, recited Hanuman Chalisa daily, and went to Connaught Place every Tuesday for the darshan of Hanuman Ji at the famous and ancient temple of the god, located opposite the Delhi Coffee House near the Rivoli Cinema Hall. I also began to visit the temple on Tuesdays and roam around the throbbing heart of the city with him.

Mr. Gupta had two grown-up daughters. His wife, a teacher who gave private tuition at her residence, earned enough to run the family. After working for various reputed names for several years,

Mr. Gupta stopped working on a full-time basis for the past couple of years due to his advanced age and his inability to work under anyone's supervision, although he continued to work on a freelance basis and had a few loyal clients who gave him work sometimes.

However, since he couldn't contribute to his family on a regular basis, he didn't get the respect and love that he expected from his wife and daughters, who mostly ignored him and treated him as a burden and drain on their financial resources, forgetting it was he who had run the family for more than 20 years earlier when he was employed, in a full-time capacity, with some of the most reputed publications, including 'Business Today' and 'Statesman.'

As he didn't get the love and respect that he expected and deserved from his family, he was always bitter and frustrated and spent most of his time outside of his house visiting exhibitions and seminars across the city on some specific occasions, accompanied by me. I looked forward to exploring the city and its many attractions with him.

Mr. Gupta remained an important part of my life for close to 18 years, guided me through various ups and downs of my life, and showed me the right path of my life and career, like a true well-wisher. Whenever I went off-track or was about to do something that wasn't morally right or lawfully inappropriate, he strongly rebuked me and advised me to behave in a responsible and mature manner. On such occasions, he addressed me in a sharp voice with a gesture of irritation, and he used to say, "You are a Brahmin and from a good family. You shouldn't do things that don't do justice to your high caste and background." He knew that my late father was an ex-army man and my late mother was a retired school principal.

He wasn't only my senior and well-wisher but also, like my own elder brother in Delhi, we spoke almost on a daily basis on the phone and met nearly every week. And when I didn't hear from him for almost a week, I became worried and called him. But there was no response. I called him again the next day, but this time around, too, I received no response. I dropped a message, but that also didn't bring any return messages.

"Perhaps he is busy; he will get back to me when he is free," I thought and soon forgot about the whole incident. Nearly a week had passed, but I still didn't hear anything from him. A little alarmed now, I prayed to God for his well-being and hoped everything was fine with him. I knew that he was on medicine as he had a weak heart. I had a feeling that one day he would find himself in a medical emergency. Still, I wasn't prepared for what I learned on that hot summer day.

I was about to board my train from Patna that day (I had gone to meet my brother and his family) when I received a WhatsApp message from Gupta Ji's number. It was brief. "Our father, Kanishka Gupta, is no more. He died yesterday peacefully in the early hours." I was stunned and refused to believe what I had just read on the flickering mobile phone screen. I checked the message again in dismay, hoping against hope that I had read it all wrong, but the message was the same.

In a state of panic, I immediately shot back a message to cross-check. "What happened? I am shocked!" Soon, I received a call from the other side. However, this time around, it wasn't the reassuring and dignified voice of Mr. Gupta; it was that of a young girl. "I am his younger daughter, Kavita. Papa passed away yesterday morning."

I knew that Kavita was Mr. Gupta's elder daughter. My mind went blank; for some time, it couldn't process the news. I kept wondering how Mr. Gupta could die so suddenly. He seemed quite well the other day when we met over a cup of coffee in New Ashok Nagar. After resigning from my previous company about a year ago, I started working for a building industry-based start-up. It was run by a group of five young people who frequently fought like dogs over petty issues. Though this sometimes pissed me off, and I clenched my fist with anger since they paid me well and respected me for the talent they believed I had, their strange, unprofessional behaviour didn't bother me much.

As if Mr. Gupta's daughter had read my thoughts, she articulated quietly, as if in a whisper, "'He was a heart patient." Though I knew Mr. Gupta was a heart patient and was in his late 50s, I didn't know that he would leave suddenly, as he was quite particular about taking his medicines on time. On getting no response from me, she said, "I will share Mummy's number with you; please speak to her and find out more." She disconnected after this, as by now, she had perhaps figured out that I was very close to her father, and so the news of his sudden death had traumatised me and left me speechless. By now, she had also perhaps learned that I was the same person with whom her father conversed almost daily and whom he met nearly every week.

The news of Mr. Gupta's sudden death had indeed badly unhinged me. For almost half an hour, I looked around strangely, and then, taking a deep, troubled breath, I began to walk to and from with folded arms, pensive and depressed, at the railway platform. This continued for almost half an hour. Then suddenly, the public address system of the railway station blared, "Vikaramshila is about to arrive at platform No. 4."

Soon, the train snaked its way in and came to a halt after some time. Everyone on the overflowing platform began to shout, jostle, and push their way towards the different coaches of the long, serpentine train. Lost in my thoughts, I, too, moved slowly towards my coach. After some difficulty, I located my berth, which was next to the aisle. Placing my bag on it, I sat on it in a highly agitated state. Soon, the super-fast train was moving towards its destination at a rapid speed.

I reached Delhi the next morning and arrived at my place a little depressed. For many days, I remained in a state of violent agitation. With Mr. Gupta's sudden exit from my life, I lost my best friend, guide, and emotional support in Delhi. Throughout the almost two decades of my life in Delhi, he was the one I turned to most often whenever I needed some sane advice and emotional support during my tough times.

It was he who helped and guided me with numerous practical pieces of advice to help me navigate through the choppy and difficult waters of my unruly life and unhinged existence. It was he who advised me to do regular jobs to restore sanity and order to my life, which had gone off-track after the twin deaths of my mother and father. It was he who advised me on how to cope with the difficult times in the wake of my painful separation from my former wife. It was he who repeatedly advised me to stay away from all kinds of wrong people.

I knew that without Mr. Gupta around, it would be difficult for me to continue with my daily life normally. After the deaths of my mother and father, there was hardly anyone I felt close to in my family. My elder sister was a pale shadow of what mother and father were for me, even though she sometimes, genuinely and honestly, tried her best to fill the big vacuum left by their sudden departure. But her efforts mostly fell short of my expectations and needs.

I don't know, but this was perhaps because she had her own large family with six grown-up kids to look after. After his retirement from active service, my brother-in-law (her husband), a rustic retired constable in his early 60s, had begun to live in his ancestral village with his younger brother and his family, away from the maddening crowds and chaos of the bustling and overcrowded Patna City, and he didn't seem concerned about his children and my sister.

My sister stayed in Patna City as three of her kids were at the time studying in the region. My brother-in-law had a small house in the city, apart from the one that he had in the remote village of Arrah. As if to justify his decision to live in his village, away from his wife and children, he often publicly claimed that he felt suffocated in the big city and was more comfortable and at peace in his village. Though I believed he was right in a way, I had a suspicion that there was more to it than what met the eye.

"Why and how can a person not miss his own wife and children and live happily with his younger brother and his well-endowed young wife in a somewhat cut-off village?" My fertile imagination and practical mind often whispered uncomfortable things into my ears whenever I thought about him, but I didn't raise the issue before my simple-minded sister. I felt it would have sown the seeds of suspicion in her impressionable mind, and she would have become badly disturbed and lost her peace of mind.

Thanks to Mr. Gupta's sudden exit from my life, I continued to feel low and listless for several weeks. When I recovered, after a couple of weeks, I started looking for opportunities in my profession, and soon I got a job nearby with a start-up in Janakpuri, West Delhi. I immediately joined it as a copywriter. It was run by two young people from Bihar in their early 30s and was located in the crowded District Centre on the sixth floor.

Although my new job didn't pay me well, it kept me fruitfully occupied for 5 days in a week. To keep my mind from slipping back into a state of hopelessness and negativity, on the weekends, I simultaneously began to catch up with some of my old acquaintances and friends with whom I had lost contact earlier. Thanks to my new job and social contacts, I began to feel better gradually. My head was fresher now, and I was calmer than I had been for the last 3 months after the unexpected death of Mr. Gupta. Before long, the spring was back in my feet, and I had begun to sip life sip-by-sip again.

Part V

XIX

The Outbreak of COVID

Life was finally on track, and everything appeared to be fine now. I even began smelling the sweet fragrance of hope. But my joy was short-lived. Hardly a few months had passed when newspapers and TV news channels began publishing and telecasting unheard news—news of deaths and destruction, news of lethal sickness and hopelessness, news of a dark present and a darker tomorrow.

It was during 2020 that the world learned that a new, mysterious virus that spread fast and was unknown till now with no cure was spreading fast across the world through air and other contacts, leaving in its wake dead bodies and incurably sick and frightened patients. The name given to the new messenger of death was COVID-19. The lethal virus, with its source of origin in China, soon had almost every part of the country in its grips.

Delhi, the capital with a high number of floating migrant people, became one of the worst-hit areas. The virus that began slowly seeping into the country from the porous borders soon infected almost every sixth or seventh person in the capital. The ill-equipped and understaffed city hospitals, as a result, got swamped with sick and dying people.

To control the new, alarming situation and prevent the spread of the lethal virus, the government clamped lockdowns in quick succession, shutting down all commercial and even most non-commercial activities in the city and across the country without any proper planning or thought. The markets and other public places were either fully or partially shut down, causing serious problems for the common people, who, in the new situation of hopelessness and fear, didn't have access to even food, groceries, and other utility stuff, and they began to suffer.

While the count of virus-infected dead bodies began to spiral across the city hospitals and mortuaries, the count of people who died due to the darkness of the ensuing uncertainty, chaos, and lack of food in many cases also began to head north in equal numbers. Besides, during the COVID phase, Work from Home (WFH) became the norm, and like thousands of other office goers, I, too, got confined to my house. The joy that had come to me after a long time of despair and despondency vanished into thin air, and I had a difficult time keeping my wandering and idyllic thoughts in check.

Wherever I went on certain occasions, in the evenings, to escape the notice of the law enforcement agencies and people, I saw listless and lifeless souls, peeping out of closed doors and windows, looking vacantly without a purpose, at a distance. It seemed the world would come to an end before long. Heartbreaking cries of distressed and distraught people rent the air, and several people whom I had known personally perished in the meantime. In the locality where I lived, there was hardly a family that didn't lose someone near and dear. I also didn't escape unscathed. I lost some of my distant family members back home and a few of my office colleagues as well. The virus continued to create havoc and leave dead bodies in its wake.

Interestingly, the pandemic brought out both the best and the worst in the common people. While it was heartening and inspiring to observe that many people during the tough and testing time came forward to lend a helping hand to the needy and the distressed by opening free food and other community services for the poor, there was also no dearth of those who revealed their true colours and became hyperactive to make hay while the sun of misery and deprivation, not to mention death, shone brightly.

To help feed the hungry and the jobless, the government began to distribute free food twice a day at the local community centres and government-run schools. Hordes of hungry and poor people who dressed appallingly thronged such places, hoping to get food. However, most of them returned empty-handed and hungry, as by the time their number came, there was no food left as it had been grabbed mainly by those with enough money to survive without the government's support and help. Much to my horror and surprise, I noticed that numerous affluent and capable people had become regulars at such places, and they carried away the food in large utensils and even canisters that were meant for the poor and the hungry.

I felt horrified and disgusted when I noticed one of my immediate neighbours going daily to the nearby food distribution centre, a government co-ed senior secondary school, and returning with big steel utensils and canisters spilling with steaming khichdi (rice and pulse preparation), rice, dal (pulses), and sabzi (vegetables). The concerned gentleman was quite well-off, a retired government employee who received a handsome pension. He had both a car and a scooter, and both of two children--a grown-up boy with curly hair and a grown-up, fat girl employed with the South Delhi-based AIIMS Hospital. They seemed to earn fairly well. I often noticed that they partied late into the night with their friends and drank freely on such occasions.

I found it difficult to understand why they were religiously grabbing the food meant for the poor, the hungry, and the distressed. Their greed and behaviour irritated me to no end and made me recoil with anger and disgust. And, so, I tried to do something to make them understand that what they were doing unapologetically wasn't right at such a time. But since I couldn't tell them in their face not to do what they were busy doing, I thought of another way to drive the message home.

I began staring at them with a crooked and malignant smile whenever I noticed them returning to their house with food brought from the free food distribution centre. I wrongly believed that it would embarrass them and dissuade them from undertaking their unethical excursions twice daily. However, I was disappointed when I noticed that my efforts had little or no effect on their activities. The gentleman and his family, like many others, continued to gobble up the food meant for the poor and the hungry with a dogged and 'I care a damn' determination.

XX

Arrival of the Two Sisters

During the COVID phase, she crossed my path in the most unexpected of ways. I had no idea then that I was courting danger, yet again, and that this time around, I wouldn't be able to escape easily and unhurt.

Ria, as I learned later, had three sisters and no brother, and she stayed in a rented apartment in an expendable small DDA flat with her parents. She was around 24, fair, slim, unmarried, and the second eldest of the four siblings, and possibly the most beautiful as well.

The first time I saw her was when the pandemic had just started and there were plans by the government to impose a lockdown. She was extremely fair and of medium height. She ran a beauty parlour next to the place where I lived. At that time, she had just opened the shutters of her main road-facing ground floor parlour and was fervently busy dusting and cleaning the place with a broom. She was sweating, and drops of perspiration stood out on her fair forehead, making her look fairer and more appealing.

After my separation from my former wife and later the exit of Sheela from my life, I had been feeling a little low. Men can't live without women. They may find women troublesome species, who lose no opportunity to fleece and trouble them at the slightest of opportunities, but take a woman out of a man's life, and he will become miserable. She could be the same person who may have even threatened to put him on bars or made life a living hell for him. But still, a man feels good and complete only when she is around to comfort him and feed him the 'nectar of life.' When she leaves, due to some reasons, he becomes parched, and afterwards, like a thirsty papiha (the familiar hawk-cuckoo, commonly known as the brain fever bird, is a medium-sized cuckoo resident in South Asia), he keeps looking for water in a highly agitated state.

Ria was a childlike and dew-fresh girl who hadn't much seen the world. One reason for this could be that she was quite young and unmarried. She was almost 15 years younger than me and sometimes looked like an innocent, lost child with a baby-like pout. I don't remember, in detail, how we came closer, but soon we had become friends and started calling each other and exchanging messages almost on a daily basis. Before long, she began to share almost everything about her troubled life and non-caring family. She told me that she had a boyfriend from Rohini, Delhi, whom she hoped to marry one day when he had finally settled down. However, at the same time, for some vague reasons, she didn't seem certain if he was the right person for her. One reason could be that he was unemployed.

Over a period of time, she introduced me to her parents and sisters. She had an elder sister named Deepika, who was married to a person and employed as a cook with an eatery in Gurugram, with whom she wasn't very happy. Deepika was around 28 with a body that begged to be laid on and kneaded brutally. She seemed to have seen the world. Unlike Ria, she was fairly mature and worldly-wise.

Ria's two younger sisters were below the age of the age of 19 and studied at a local school. Her father ran a small grocery shop in the nearby market, and her half-Nepali and half-Garhwali mother worked in a nursing home in Green Park, South Delhi, as an attendant.

Overall, her family was quite poor, and they stayed in a one-bedroom rented apartment on the second floor of a building owned by an elderly ex-army Jat who appeared to be suspicious of them and didn't seem too comfortable having them around for some unexplained reasons. When he saw me for the first time with Ria, he gave me a hard, contemptuous look that seemed to say, 'I know what has brought you here, you sex-starved asshole!'

Over a period of time, I lost track of Ria and her family, as she had shut down her beauty parlour and vanished suddenly without even informing me. "Maybe she has gotten married and is now busy with her new life." I was a little distraught. However, since I didn't want to disturb her and create any sort of problems in her new life with my unnecessary interference, I didn't think much about her, and soon I forgot her. However, out of curiosity, after a few months, I tried connecting with her, but I found her mobile switched off. "Maybe she has changed her number intentionally as she isn't keen to keep contact with her past," I mulled with a bitter smile.

But I was wrong. That day, during the month of March, just before Holi, while I was having my breakfast at a roadside restaurant, I received a call from an unknown number. The caller was none other than Ria. Pleasingly surprised at the unexpected turn of events, I asked her where she had disappeared all of a sudden. She responded by saying that she had tied the knot and was living with her husband and in-laws in the Safdarjung Area of South Delhi, near the now-closed Uphar Cinema, close to the famed Rajinder Dhaba that is popular across Delhi for its lip-smacking non-vegetarian stuff, including Chicken Korma, Mutton Korma, and the melt-in-the-mouth Gulauti Kabab.

When I congratulated her on marrying her boyfriend, she didn't seem very pleased. Sensing something was wrong, I asked her gently, without sounding too intrusive, what the matter was. She responded with a sigh that she had hurriedly gotten married to a person whom she had been in contact with since her childhood. Then, after a brief pause, she added that he wasn't the same person about whom she had spoken to me earlier. When she realised that I had become confused, she said, "The person whom I knew and about whom I had a discussion with you sometime back was already married, and so I ditched him at the last moment. "

"You did the right thing," I said. But she cut me short abruptly, crying, "I don't know!" Then she added hurriedly that life hadn't treated her fairly. A little worried, I asked what the matter was, and she said, "Can we meet the next day?" Since I too wanted to meet her and catch up with her, for old time's sake, I agreed right away.

Later in the evening, I strangely found myself a little perked up and happy for some unknown, unexplained reasons. I began to whistle with a broad smile. At that time, I was standing on the balcony of my house. It was around 6 p.m., and the evening was about to close in. Then suddenly, I noticed my immediate neighbour's young wife standing on the balcony of her house, located right opposite my house, and looking at me in a rather strange way. The chubby-baby-faced woman with flowing brown hair caressed her generous hips when she walked slowly. She seemed to be a little frightened and on her guard.

When our eyes briefly met for a moment, I immediately looked away, a little embarrassed, and, in a hurry, turned my back on her, leaving the balcony of my house. "Perhaps she had misread the situation and had thought that I was making a pass at finding her alone." I thought later of horror. Soon, I forgot about the incident when my mind drifted again towards Ria. I became buoyed once again at the thought of the endless positive possibilities that seemed to await me with open arms just around the corner.

Ria called me the next day, saying she was in my area and had come to meet her parents. When I asked her to meet me at my place, she agreed right away, though it surprised me in no way as she was now a married person and had gotten married just a couple of days ago. In a state of excitement, I dressed up appropriately for the occasion and then drove my bike to the place about which she had informed me earlier that she would wait for me after leaving her bus. When I reached the spot, I was 15 minutes late, and she was already waiting, scanning the area with anxious eyes. She was in a blue pair of jeans and a white top with laces.

"Oh, she is looking for me!" I was overjoyed. When she found me, her eyes lit up with excitement and happiness. After exchanging pleasantries with her, I asked her to hop on my bike. She seemed to be a little hesitant initially, but when I told her with a twinkle in my eyes that I wouldn't kidnap her, as she had already been taken, she relented sheepishly, and soon I was driving my bike on the smooth Dwarka roads, and she was riding pillion. Her slim body was tightly pressed against my body. She seemed to be a little uncomfortable with the seat of my Apache Bike, which pushed her towards me with every twist and turn. I wanted to give her a ride and let her breathe in some fresh air before I brought her to my flat.

When we finally reached my house, I was relieved to see none of my neighbours around in the afternoon, and most of the ladies in the neighbourhood seemed to be busy cooking food in their kitchens while the men were away from their houses for jobs and business purposes. While ascending the stairs of my bachelor floor with Ria, I was quite excited and could even hear my heart beating excitedly with anticipation. After a very long time, I was alone with a woman. Ria appeared to be a little nervous in the beginning, but after we had settled comfortably inside, she opened up a little and became relaxed.

We spent close to two hours in each other's company, during which we had tea prepared by her and hot samosas that I bought on my way. Then, she began sharing her family and other details. She told me that she wasn't happy with her husband and her in-laws, as they were uncaring and didn't treat her well. She seemed to be especially bitter about her husband, a Thapa from Nepal. When I asked how she had married into a Nepali family, she didn't respond for some time. Then she said with a lot of anger that she got married into a Thapa family because she was cursed and destined to live unhappily throughout her life.

Then, she suddenly began to sob, hiding her face in her handkerchief. This startled me, and if by an impulse, I immediately began to comfort her with soothing words. "Don't worry—everything will be fine." "No!" she responded with a little vehemence and continued to air her grief passionately. By now, I was a little confused and even worried, as I feared her cries might be heard outside and my neighbours might imagine things.

As if to prevent such a possibility, I took hold of her hands and pressed them gently, cooing soothing and reassuring words into her ears. "Please don't cry; I can't see you crying like this." This, as if by magic, reined in her tears, and she stopped crying. Then, wiping her tears with her little cotton handkerchief, she said, a little embarrassed but with sad eyes, "Sorry for troubling you with my grief."

She left me half an hour after clearing the table and cleaning the utensils, despite my protests. "You live alone, right? From now on, you don't have to either cook or do the usual household chores on your own. I will do it for you whenever I come to meet my parents." She cried, looking at me deeply as if trying to study my reactions.

I was overjoyed. By the time I dropped her at her parent's place, we had some unsaid and unarticulated understanding of sorts between us that said, 'We would be for each other from now onwards and fulfil each other's needs with love.'

From that day on, Ria started visiting me whenever she came from her in-law's place in South Delhi to visit her family. A month passed, during which we became quite close, and it was inevitable that we would cross the remaining barriers one day. However, as I had a bad experience in the past with some of the women who had crossed my path, I tried to keep my wandering impulses in check. But it's difficult to keep the surging water of a frothing river in check for long, even if you have built towering dams to stop the flow of water at some points. One day, the river will go out of control and break all natural and man-made barriers to flood and swamp whatever comes in its way before losing its ferocious energy and tapering off to its earlier state.

It was a rather hot summer day that day. She was with me at my place when suddenly I had a surge of hormones. I lost control over myself, and before I or she knew what I was up to, I had her slim body in my arms and was kissing her like a man possessed. The colour rushed to her face, but since she seemed to have been waiting for such an eventuality for so long, she comfortably melted in my burning embrace and left herself loose in my arms.

Ria wasn't tall; at 5'2, she looked like a doll, and I had no difficulties in letting my unruly desires shepherd my moves and pin her on my study table. Soon, we were swimming in the ocean of pleasure, and she constantly encouraged me sweetly and passionately. She accommodated me easily and welcomed me with a smile that fired my longing further, and before long, I was chugging into the dark and slippery tunnel of passion with a rampaging speed.

Before leaving me that day, Ria sought Rs. 10, 000 from me, saying she needed it as her husband and the in-laws never gave her any money, and she so often faced a lot of difficulties meeting her needs. I gave her the money without thinking twice, as I was hooked by now and was looking at her with a long-term goal. Much more strangely, she had asked for money soon after we had consumed each other. Even though the timing left me feeling a little strange, I didn't think much about this, as after so many days, I had a woman. Ria called me again after 3–4 days, and we met, like before. Before leaving me, she asked for a second time, and I gave her Rs 5,000 this time around.

From that day onwards, whenever she came to visit me and after we had consumed each other, she sought money from me, and I gave her what she wanted; though, over a period of time, I began to feel a little uneasy and uncomfortable with her greed and non-stop demands and even began thinking of looking for an alternative.

I got that alternative, surprisingly, from Ria herself when, one day, she introduced me to her elder sister. I had heard about her sister and knew she was very disturbed with her husband, as he didn't fulfil his duties and was quarrelsome. I had learned from Ria that her sister's husband had made her life a living hell, and she was always irritated by this. Ria asked me to guide and console her sister. "You are a mature and wise man. I am sure you will help and guide Didi well the way you have helped and guided me."

XXI

The Naked Desire

When I saw Deepika for the first time, I was surprised to notice a big difference between the two sisters. Unlike Ria, Deepika was well-endowed and rather stoutly built. She was in her late 20s and was fashionably dressed. She wasn't fair, like Ria, though she looked more feminine and inviting. By profession, she was a physiotherapist; she didn't have a set-up of her own, though. She often visited her female clients and gave them physiotherapy sessions at their homes.

She seemed to have seen the world more and knew how to ensnare men with her charms. She also knew that her sister was in a relationship with me. So, in the beginning, Deepika maintained a respectable distance from her sister's boyfriend, i.e., me, and treated me with respect. I, too, behaved as a man behaves with his wife's or girlfriend's elder; I gave her the respect that I felt was appropriate in the given situation, knowing well that sisters mostly share almost everything with each other, though with the passage of time I found myself gradually slipping towards Deepika's womanly charm and attraction. That she was married and living separately from her husband only fuelled the fire burning inside me and made her more attractive in my roving eyes.

From my experience, I know that the women living separately from their husbands are dangerously hungry for male company, and when they finally get a chance, they go all guns blazing, and they give such an experience to their partners that the latter never forget throughout their lives. Much inspired, I often guided and helped Deepika with small, regular things, like looking for a cheap house for rental purposes and getting her four year old kid admitted to a nearby nursery. Soon, she became so dependent on me that she began to call me for small things and seek my advice on almost everything.

Like Ria, Deepika loved my voice and the way I advised her to deal with her husband and other unanticipated 'disturbances' of her life--calmly and patiently. She seemed to be a lost soul who appeared to have a constant need for a mature person around who could give her disturbed and directionless life the right meaning and the right direction. I guided and advised her in the best way possible, hoping to make her life better. I didn't know at that time that I was getting sucked into her little world.

I began visiting her at her place almost every week, and her family became quite comfortable with my presence in their house, even at odd hours, throughout this period. However, I took care not to visit them when Ria was around. I knew that sibling rivalry between the two sisters would have made the situation complicated, and I may have ended up losing both.

After some time, Deepika even began to treat me as her husband and introduced me to her new landlord as her 'husband', as her actual husband had by then almost been cut off from her life, and his visits to her had become rare. There were even talks of a likely divorce between the two. I often wondered if I was the reason behind this development, but then I consoled myself by thinking that there were irreparable differences and an unbridgeable chasm between the estranged couple for a long time—right from the time

I was not even a part of Deepika's life—and so I shouldn't take the blame for their separation.

I also began to pick up Deepika from her place and drop her off wherever she wanted during that period. All through this phase, though we had become quite intimate, we hadn't yet cemented our relationship with the inevitable. No wonder there's still that teasing gap between us, which wasn't there between her younger sister Ria and me. We knew that it was just a matter of time before the barrier broke; we became truly intimate and became 'husband' and 'wife' in the real sense.

That time came soon.

One day, sometime during the month of April, she called me late in the evening and asked me to pick her up from her residence as she was keen to have piping hot momos at a nice place in Dwarka. "I am dying to have a steaming plate of Momos. Do you know any place in Dwarka where I can have Momos to my heart's content?" Since I knew many such places, I immediately responded with 'Yes,' and then I picked her up at the scheduled time and drove her to the throbbing and busy Central Market of Dwarka.

There, I ordered a plate of steaming hot chicken momos for her that she ate with childlike enthusiasm before washing the food with a can of chilled Pepsi. After enjoying the hot food and the cold beverage, she asked me to drive her through Dwarka. "Give me a nice experience; I want to fly!" She appeared to be in a good mood and had started humming a famous romantic tune from a popular Shahid and Kareena Kapoor Bollywood movie—*Na, Hai Yeh Pana...Na Khona He Hai...Tera Na Hona, Jaane...Kuyn Hona He Hai.*

Palpitating with an unknown desire, I drove her leisurely through the coal-black and smooth roads of the sub-city aimlessly for about an hour, during which she, riding pillion, clung to me like a reed.

Before long, I was on fire, and my body began to burn with an unknown desire. I didn't know what to do or how to get her to do what was consuming me like a raging inferno.

"What if she creates a scene before others and publicly humiliates me for taking advantage of her and later informs Ria?" While I battled with all such disturbing thoughts and drove my blue 160 CC Apache aimlessly across the many sectors of Dwarka, she suddenly asked me if I had a nice, private place tucked somewhere where we could spend some quality time in complete privacy. This thrilled me greatly, as now it was crystal clear that she was on fire, like me, and wanted an outlet to douse the raging flames of passion.

As luck would have it, I had the keys to one of my friend's unoccupied flats. It was located on the second floor of a sparsely populated DDA locality in Dwarka. I drove my bike straight to the place and took her there. I noticed that my heart was now throbbing slowly and violently with excitement. She was equally excited and had a mysterious and all-knowing twinkle in her eyes. She appeared to clearly know what lay in store and what I was up to. But perhaps she hadn't thought that the place would be totally empty and not even have a bed or a chair on which she could relax for some time before she gradually opened up. When I opened the lock to the flat and threw the doors wide open, exposing the dark and completely empty room inside, she looked uncomfortable, confused, and a little demoralised as well, wondering where I had brought her.

Sensing her discomfort and reluctance, I relaxed her by taking her in my arms and planting a kiss on her half-open lips. Her lips were thick and reminded me of dark brown chocolates that I sometimes saw pretty girls devouring in the commercials. By now, Deepika seemed to be suffering from a fever, and her body was literally burning. Had I not taken the initiative, perhaps she would have never come so far with me. After shutting the door, I embraced her burning body and began to fervently kiss her body. Neck, lips, forehead, eyes, and the middle of her breasts—not a single area of her pleasingly plump body remained un-kissed, un-teased, un-explored, and un-devoured. My mad actions had an electrifying effect on her, and she got dangerously aroused. She started moaning and tearing my clothes away as if she were possessed.

Without wasting any more time and dusting the dirty floor with a dirty abandoned piece of newspaper that I located in the corner of the pigeon-infected flat, I gently put her on the floor. And then I tore her flexible jeans wide open with lightning speed and began to devour her with frenzied energy and unimaginable madness. She started to enjoy my madness—and that of hers—so much that she started moaning loudly, and this panicked a pair of pigeons that so far had been sitting quietly in the cupboard of the dark kitchen and watching the unexpected, unfolding drama with curiosity.

The pair felt threatened and began to look for an escape route. As the house was securely shut, they couldn't find any escape route. Much terrified by now, they began to quickly flutter from one corner to another, dropping their little feathers and pigeon droppings everywhere across the room. Some of their feathers and droppings fell on Deepika's naked and profusely sweating body and clung to it, making her look like a naked jungle goddess decked with white and grey feathers and yellow pigeon droppings. But unmindful of the dirt and the frenzied, frightened fluttering of the terrified birds, I kept on devouring her with all my raw energy and madness and scaling the Himalayan heights of pleasure.

After about half an hour, we exploded almost at the same time and lay limp and sweating badly in each other's arms for some time. We were drenched with each other's sweat and bodily juices. Then, getting up slowly with a smile, Deepika wiped herself and me clean with a piece of cotton cloth that she mysteriously fished out of her purse. She then dressed quietly in the dim light of the room, which by now had become a little dark as the sun had sunk into the distant horizon and the night was about to close in.

While driving towards her house that day, I experienced a unique sense of calm and euphoria, which I hadn't experienced with any of the many women with whom I had a physical relationship so far. Deepika seemed to be equally happy and satisfied; she had placed her head gently on my back while my bike sped speedily on the shiny, black roads of the sub-city.

I dropped her off at her place after around 30 minutes. Before leaving me, she quickly planted a kiss on my unsuspecting face, and before I could grab her and smother her with innumerable kisses in return, she had vanished in the thick weekly market crowd. It was Tuesday, the day of the weekly bazaar in the area. Hawkers were busy selling their wares and all kinds of stuff, including fruits, vegetables, clothes, spices, and ladies' undergarments, which were on full display for the thronging crowd of local shoppers.

Cutting my way through the stream of the crowd with great dexterity, I returned to my place feeling blessed and on top of the world. My face beamed with happiness and satisfaction. I had no complaints about life. I was a happy and fully satisfied man; a state of extraordinary excitement seemed to envelop my being and bathe it with a pleasurable sensation. God appeared to be kind and generous with me.

From that day onwards, I frequently picked her up from her house, and we spent several hours happily together, lost in each other's arms. She gave me much more pleasure than what I had received so far from either Ria, or, for that matter, any other woman in my life. And so, I unknowingly became a little possessive of her and began to give Ria less time, all the while spending more time with Deepika.

XXII

Another Dangerous Situation

This proved to be costly in the long run and alienated me from Ria. In the meantime, Deepika, who already had many admirers, began to look beyond me and use her charm in the most imaginative ways possible to ensnare those who caught her fancy and who, she believed, would help her lead a good life, free from any wants.

One major reason why she, perhaps, had lost interest in me after some time was that I wasn't spending money on her and her family the way she wanted. Adding further to her growing disinterest in me was that I had become quite possessive of her of late. She felt suffocated. When she could take it no more, she dumped me coldly and suddenly—almost in the same way as I had dumped her sister, Ria, earlier.

There was another important reason for her losing interest in me all of a sudden and avoiding me. A gym owner had come into her life; he was a muscular jat boy from Najafgarh (Delhi), richer, and better looking. Besides, while he splurged money on her generously, I didn't. So, in her new scheme of things, I had become a misfit; now, there was no place for me in her life. I protested, as by now she had become my weakness, and I was in love with her sensuous body and its many hidden charms. Her anger increased when she realised that I had clung to her like a pest and wasn't allowing her to break free.

Seething with anger, she started to ignore me openly, not answer my repeated calls, and discourage my overtures in every way possible. However, when she realised that I wasn't ready to let her go, she lost her cool. And one day, in a fit of anger, she filed a police complaint against me, alleging that I was stalking and harassing her. Ria-who, so far, had been watching the unfolding drama and smarting under my continued neglect, joined her. And, prodded by Deepika, she also filed a similar police complaint against me at the same police station.

Now, I was in a critical situation. Two young girls from the same family had approached the police against me with a similar and serious complaint. To make matters worse, Deepika also blamed me for the troubles in her marital life. She had been divorced lately, and she alleged that I was the main reason behind her separation from her husband. It was an altogether different matter that her husband had divorced her, as he had caught her red-handed, as I learned later, with some people on a couple of occasions.

But when the police didn't move against me since, on the advice of a lawyer friend, I had already greased their palms and convinced them that the two sisters were targeting me unfairly after fleecing me for long—they approached a local politician who was also a notorious muscleman of her area. The man, called Ballu Tokas, had contact with all kinds of people, including the local goons.

The dark-complexioned and half-bald Bali, who had a throaty voice, had his own reasons to come to the two sisters' rescue and go after me. The 60-year-old man had a suspicion that I was in a physical relationship with the two sisters, whom he openly coveted. So, he was furious and waited for his time to teach me a lesson for coming in his way and snatching away from him what he felt was his. When the two women sought his help and asked him to teach me a lesson, he was elated. He used his contacts and goons against me to make the two women happy. He began to send all kinds of notorious people to my place; on at least two occasions, I had strange-looking visitors at my house late in the evenings.

Fortunately, on both occasions, I wasn't at home. I learned about them from my neighbour when I returned from my office later. "Two people were looking for you. One of them carried a hockey stick with him," informed my neighbour Mr. Sharma, a retired bank officer, when I returned one day from my office late in the evening. Then, bringing his mouth close to my ear, he whispered, casting a troubled look around as if he were afraid of somebody, "They didn't look like hockey players." A little alarmed, I thanked him for the information and then opened the lock to my house and shut it securely afterwards from inside.

Almost a week passed with no untoward incident. I had almost forgotten the visits by the strange-looking people when one day the unexpected happened and my worst fears came true. It was raining that day. I had just returned from my office, drenched and dead-tired, and was about to open the door of my third-floor apartment when I heard a hoarse voice from behind. However, before I could turn my head in that direction and find out who was there, someone stuck something sharp into my left thigh from behind. I immediately drew back in panic. But by then, it was too late. The object was a sharp-edged knife, and it had done its work; my blue Levi Jeans had gotten drenched with blood, and a searing pain was shooting through my entire body.

However, before I could react and do anything or make even a feeble effort to get hold of the person who had attacked me right in front of my flat, he vanished in the dimly lit corridor of the building. All I could hear was the feeble, dying sound of his steps on the stairs far away. I gasped for breath, afterwards clenching my teeth with pain.

With great difficulty, I somehow opened the door to my flat and then collapsed into the nearest chair, worn with pain and weak from the protracted bleeding. After a while, when I somehow regained my senses and came to myself, I took out my mobile phone from the pocket of my half-wet jeans, and then, wiping the wet surface of the phone with the cushion cover of the nearby sofa, I called the security guard of my society.

The security guard—a dark-complexioned, gutka-chewing man in his early 40s—came at once. When he saw me in such a state for a couple of minutes, he gazed about him with his mouth open as if he had seen a man bleeding profusely for the first time in his life. Then, when he finally realised what he was expected to do in such a situation, he took out his shiny Nokia 800 from his left pocket. Then, he quickly made some frantic calls. Soon, two senior RWA members of the society, President Mishra and Treasurer Gandhi, turned up at my place.

On learning what had taken place, they called the local doctor right away. The doctor, a tall man in his early 50s with thin hair, dressed my wound with a bandage and afterwards gave me a tetanus injection. Before leaving, he asked me to come for a follow-up after two days. He also gave me some blue and red pills to take twice a day for the next five days, saying they were antibiotics and painkillers. He assured me and the people around me that I would be fine soon.

Later that day, a sharp-eyed policeman—a sub-inspector with a thin moustache and hawk-like nose—visited me as the RWA had also dialled the local police and informed them about the incident. After sinking into the sofa in my drawing room and drinking the ginger tea that my maid had prepared for us, he asked me all sorts of strange questions. "Who attacked you? Did you suspect someone? Do you have any enmity with someone? Are you in a relationship with someone? How long have you been staying here?"

Since I had no answers, I gave him only vague answers, evading his sharp and distrusting eyes all the while. Then I turned my head away and dropped my eyes to discourage him from pestering me with more uncomfortable questions. For a few minutes, he waited patiently, hoping to get some information from me, all the while looking at me with an indescribable gaze. However, when he finally realised that I was in no mood to answer his questions, he left me, informing me that he would file an FIR and would soon begin a formal inquiry. For some reason, I hadn't told him about the girls and the goon known to them, as it would have brought everything out in the open, and my troubles would have perhaps increased further.

I was asked to come to the local police station several times over the next couple of weeks. But since I wasn't forthcoming, and the CCTV cameras of my society weren't working (as usual) that eventful day, the investigating officer couldn't make any headway. He soon lost interest in my case and closed it after I had given my approval for it in writing. And with this, a weight appeared to have rolled from my, and I fancy, as well as the IO's heart and mind.

Almost three months had passed, and no major event had happened. I had regained my strength that had dipped thanks to the loss of blood due to the unexpected physical assault earlier on that fateful evening. I had already forgotten the unexpected brutal attack on me, like a bad dream, when one day, I received a call from an unknown number. It was raining that day; I had just returned from my office and was leisurely sipping a hot cup of Bru coffee at that time.

The caller identified himself as Ballu Tokas. He told me that the person who had attacked me about three months ago with a knife was his man, and he had sent him to me to threaten me at the behest of Deepika and her sister, Ria. He asserted that he was sorry for what he had done, stating that the sisters had played with his sentiments and used him against me. He afterwards started hurling abuses against the girls, exclaiming that they had duped and dumped him after using him and taking a huge amount of money and favours from him. I told him disinterestedly that I had already forgotten the incident and held no grudge against him, and so he shouldn't worry. Then, without waiting for his reply, I disconnected the call.

I thanked God later for saving and shielding me against the women and their contacts. Hadn't I moved out fast and decided to sever contact with them, perhaps they would have done incalculable harm to me, using the likes of Ballu Tokas. One day, they will also pay for their sins, as I had to do later. They had wronged me and perhaps many others in a similar way. One day, a person wronged by them in a similar manner would take revenge, and their karma would bring justice for me, and for many others wronged similarly by them. On second thoughts, the blame for the mess in which I had landed lay squarely with me. I shouldn't have been a slave to my own base desires and should exercise extreme caution while dealing with such women.

To avoid repeating similar mistakes committed earlier, from that day on, I began to take extreme caution while dealing with people, especially women, and started to strictly stay away from those whom I felt could tempt me to endanger my life and destroy my peace of mind in any way. Though I did come across several situations that tested my resolve and lured me towards similar situations, I stuck to my resolve determinedly and tried my best to lead a good and virtuous life free from all such negative and dangerous people and influences.

XXIII

The Sunset of My 'Unhinged' Life

Today, I am over 55 years old with a pale face and stricken eyes. I am known in my residential society as a struggling writer and author who lives alone on the 11th floor of the 14th-floor apartment, which is almost cut off from the world and has no visitors. I had moved out of my previous accommodation soon after that eventful attack and occupied a new place on the outskirts of the city.

Despite numerous setbacks and more downs than ups in my life, life seems to be somewhat kind to me, but I still feel restless and unhinged sometimes. I don't know what life has in store for me. I don't know for how many more years I will live in this world like this. With, barring my elder sister, no one in my family around to feel for me, no one around whom I can call my family in the real sense, I have almost lost the will to live. While my body has begun to fail me, my eyes aren't doing any better and have become quite weak, of late. I also get tired rather fast these days. I have lost my appetite, too, and don't feel like eating meals twice a day. On many days, I just have a glass of milk or some fruit throughout the day.

I feel that my days are limited, and I might leave this world unexpectedly. When that happens, there will be no one to mourn my passing. If death arrives without warning, I fear my body will remain unnoticed for days, decomposing in my sparsely populated apartment, with no one aware of my demise.

The floor on which I live has four flats, the remaining being unoccupied. The old security guard, who smells horribly, will notice my absence only when he doesn't see me for many days at the end. In such a case, perhaps he would visit my flat, cursing me under his breath, and would be horrified to find my dead body. Since only the name and the number of my elder sister are in society's RWA records, they will inform her, and she will shed tears quietly in memory of her unfortunate brother, who died alone in an alien city and whose even last Hindu rites couldn't be performed. For a couple of days, she would possibly weep, cursing fate for being so cruel to her brother, who once was the most loved and pampered child of his parents and who had a quite promising life ahead earlier.

It's a dark and airless evening, and I am feeling stifled and uneasy now. The twilight has fallen, and the full moon is shining more brightly; there is a peculiar breathlessness in the air, though. As if gasping for air, I hastily go to the window of my one-bedroom flat, feel for the latch, and open it. The window opens into the society park. Fresh, cool, light air moves into the room, making me feel happy for a moment. But soon, I relapse into my old hopeless and melancholy state.

Now it's about 1:30 a.m., and I don't see a single soul stirring anywhere outside in the park or on the adjoining roads. Everything looks quiet and ghostly, bathed in the silvery moonlight. For a few minutes, I gaze into the silvery darkness in a meaningless way and dreamily. Then, for some unknown reason, I hastily close the window and sink back into my wooden chair, a little exhausted. These days, I become pale and tired very fast, though I have no idea why.

I have lived half a decade of an uneventful life, and now I have a strange feeling that something unexpected is about to happen soon. The reels of my past life float fast before my weak eyes. Some thoughts or remains of thoughts, some images float before my tired and exhausted mind. I see faces of people I had seen maybe in my childhood or bumped into somewhere once whom I would never have recollected: the dwarf mechanic from the garage located near the railway station, the pot-bellied security guard of the bank where my mother had a locker, the beautiful woman hawker with very wide hips who walked gently. The images follow one another in rapid succession, but they fade gradually.

I also see some familiar faces from my family; I see my mother and father, dead long ago, waiting for me with their open arms and a wide smile to shower me with love. I also see my elder sister bent over the stove, preparing something delicious for me. I also have a somewhat blurred and hazy glimpse of my wife, who is decked in a bright red saree (a women's piece of clothing that has an un-stitched stretch of woven fabric arranged over the body, something like a dressing gown) and is bejewelled with heavy jewellery. I also see my school life and find myself being congratulated by my friends for emerging as an undisputed winner in the boxing arena.

Now my eyelids feel heavy, but this isn't with sleep but something entirely different. I also feel a strange, burning sensation somewhere inside the left side of my chest. Now I have begun to perspire simultaneously, rather heavily, and my hair has gotten soaked with sweat, though it's the month of November and fairly cold outside.

Suddenly, I hear the stifled howling of the wind under the window. The weather seems to have changed all of a sudden. "Will it rain?" I move slowly towards the closed window. "But who cares if it rains or not?" As if irritated and a little exhausted with my own thoughts, I return and sink back into my chair in a state of agitated excitement and begin to feel uneasy. "Is the end near?" I have no idea. I hope to see the sun rising and bathing everything in its golden hue the next day, but strangely, I don't see its possibility for some unexplained reasons.

Now, the wind has started to roar outside and hammer the panes of the closed window. "It wants to enter my room. But what does it want from me?" I wonder with my eyes half-open, in a sort of reverie. "Come; tell me, what do you want? You want to say 'Goodbye,' right?" I am a little puzzled now and then doze off, thinking somewhat troubled and tired.

I sleep peacefully for half an hour or so, and then I start. In the dim light of the room, I try to look at the photographs of my parents hung on the opposite wall. On finding them looking at me with a smile, I smile back at them involuntarily. Sleep crawls towards me stealthily yet again, and my eyes close slowly. I feel good, and my head feels light. Eternal peace envelopes me in its welcoming and soothing arms. I am completely at peace with myself and the world now.

Ma, here I come!

-The End—